Praise for
The Goodbye Process

"Startling, haunting, and original. Mary Jones captures the eerie light that transfuses those often-forgotten and overlooked corners of the heart. These stories shape-shift and beguile, offering up their remarkable insights with wit and genuine style. A brilliant book of stories."

—Brandon Taylor, author of *The Late Americans*

"Jones builds enormous depth in direct, clear sentences. I found myself moved and wowed by how much she packed into a moment. Her words have these subtle magnets in them, drawing a reader close. Thrilling abundance here."

—Aimee Bender, author of *The Particular Sadness of Lemon Cake*

"Jones's delightful story collection is full of surprises—sometimes funny, often heartbreaking, always memorable."

Jill McCorkle, author of *Old Crimes: and Other Stories*

"In these exquisite and emotionally distilled stories, Jones illuminates the mysterious corners of grief and grace with poignancy and spiky humor. Her explorations of sex, sorrow, and wonder are transfixing and brilliant. This is a must-read collection."

—Mary Otis, author of *Burst*

"Keenly felt and observed, always humane, *The Goodbye Process* introduces an arresting new voice."

—Taylor Koekkoek, author of *Thrillville, USA*

The Goodbye Process

Mary Jones

Zibby Books
New York

Several of these stories previously appeared, in slightly different form, in the following publications: *EPOCH* ("From Outside I Could See"), *Faultline* ("The Next Husband Game"), *Electric Literature's Recommended Reading* ("Absences"), *New South* ("The One Who Keeps the Washcloth Cold"), *Gay Mag* ("The Widow"), *Brevity* ("The Father"), *The Hopkins Review* ("Tell Me Something New"), *Epiphany* ("We're Not So Far from There"), *Santa Monica Review* ("Thanksgiving"), *Meridian* ("Everything That's Left"), *Boston Literary Magazine* ("The Short History of Her Heart"), *Alaska Quarterly Review* ("On the Other Side of the Yard"), *The Chattahoochee Review* ("If There's Anything You Need"), *Carve* ("Customer of Size"), *The Greensboro Review* ("The Correct Way to Breathe"), and *The Indiana Review* ("Royalty").

Library of Congress Control Number: 2024931227
Paperback ISBN: 978-1-958506-62-2
Hardcover ISBN: 978-1-958506-63-9
eBook ISBN: 978-1-958506-64-6

Book design by Ursula Damm
Cover design by Anna Morrison
www.zibbymedia.com

Printed in the United States of America

10 9 8 7 6 5 4 3 2 1

For Sophie and Steve

i carry your heart with me
(i carry it in my heart)
—e. e. cummings

Contents

From Outside I Could See

We were in the living room after dinner and he took my hand and walked me to the door and opened it. "What's this?" I said. "You want me to leave?" I said. I walked through the door and he locked it. Very funny. I knocked on the door. He didn't answer. I looked through the window that looked out onto the street. From inside you could see the palm trees sway and it was surprisingly pretty. From outside I could see him quickly moving around. This was not comforting. I knocked. *Remember me?* It had been going on a little long. And anyway, we were too old for this. He did not respond to the knocks.

I sat down on the step. "Do you want to see a trick?" a neighbor boy on a skateboard said.

"No," I said.

"Watch," he said. He skated back into the road and did some kind of twirl.

It wasn't very impressive.

Inside I heard banging and when I went to the window I saw that it was boarded up.

I went to the back, to the little rock in the yard which was hollowed out and held a key. I got the key and tried it in the back door. But he had changed the lock. I tried all the windows. No use. I borrowed a ladder from the mother of the skater kid. What was I going to do? I loved him. Really loved him. I had to get in. To see him. I felt like if I just got in and if I could see him again, and if he saw me with no walls between us, it might make all the difference. He might remember that he loved me. That I was the person he said he wanted to spend his life with. The person he wanted to be the mama of his babies.

But it was too late. The second-floor windows were boarded up too. Things were secure. There was no getting in, and I knew he had supplies.

I borrowed a sleeping bag from the skater kid and I camped out on his porch. I waited. I was hungry and cold and sad and confused, but I waited. I waited for him to be done being mad. Or done being sad. Or done hating me. Or done blaming me. I waited for him to come out. To be him again. So I could be me. But he did not open the door. Months passed. Years. I was not one to give up. As I said, I really loved him. I had gotten skinny and my hair turned gray, and the kid on the skateboard grew up and went to college. And he did not come out. And I never knew what happened. Or why, or what I'd done. And every day, I kept my face turned so I could see the door, and I waited for it to open. But it did not open. And I never saw him again. Never loved again. Never anything.

THE NEXT HUSBAND GAME

We played this funny game. It wasn't a quick game, it was a game we played from the first year we were married. We'd jump in and out of it: the playing of this game was, I guess you could say, intermittently continuous. It was called: the Next Husband/Wife Game. I made it up. The only rule was, once someone had a turn, the other person had to go too, so you always had to have one ready just in case. In a sense, you had to always be thinking about it. My husband went for it as soon as I explained it to him. It was a cold night and the fire was going. We were eating Chinese food on the couch and watching *The Bachelor*.

"Easy," he said, running his fingers through his brown wavy hair. "My next wife will blow me," he said. "Every day."

It was so obvious that I almost felt sorry for him. His lack of originality. His lack of careful thought about anything. This was him to a T. I said, "My next husband will cook."

The next time was a few weeks later. We were on our way home from a friend's New Year's Eve party. It had been a bore of a night. The truth was we hated all of our friends. Every time we saw them we had to gear ourselves up to get through it. My husband came up short on enthusiasm that night. He sat in a corner sulking. "What's wrong with Joe?" everyone kept saying. "Is something going on with Joe?"

On the way home it was snowing and there were police cars everywhere. "My next husband won't be so moody," I said, looking out at the road. I was being careful with the car, driving slow. I admit there was some bite to what I said, but behind that, if you looked deeper, there was actually a loving message. *Cheer up!* I was trying to tell him. *It's New Year's Eve, for Christ's sake.*

I saw him glaring at me from the passenger seat. He was quiet for a minute. "My next wife will be twenty-one," he said.

Well, that cut to it. I was nearing forty and could see for the first time all the ways I would become ugly. There was nothing on earth more terrifying to me than a twenty-one-year-old girl. I pressed my foot on the gas, hoping to scare him. But then I remembered all the cops and slowed back down.

We kept playing through the years.

When he was on me about my spending, I said, "My next husband will make enough money."

When the house was a mess, he said, "My next wife will know how to clean."

When I was telling him about missing my mother and he was looking at his phone, I said, "My next husband will listen to me when I talk."

When I screamed at him for not emptying the dishwasher, he said, "My next wife will not be a rage-filled cunt."

I said, "My next husband will know how to turn me on and how to make me come."

He said, "I won't literally hate my next wife."

After, we got divorced. By this point, I thought it was probably for the best. I adopted a cat and started taking yoga classes.

Last week we bumped into each other at the mall and sat down for a cup of coffee. It had been many years and we were both married again, why not. "That stupid game," he said after a while. "*That* was the thing that got us."

He was as handsome as he'd ever been. Possibly even more so with the graying hair. "I was actually thinking about it the other day," I said. "I have to say I didn't follow through on any of my things. My next husband turned out to be almost the exact same kind of asshole as you," I said.

"What do you mean, 'same kind of asshole'?" he said.

"There are lots of different kinds of assholes," I said. "He just happens to be a distant and moody one like you."

"I'm sorry," he said. "I would have wanted you to find a better kind of asshole."

"Oh," I said. "You weren't so bad."

After a minute he laughed. He said that just this morning his wife had lost her mind because he forgot to wash their daughter's lunch box, then she stormed out of the house and drove off in her car. "I guess I didn't follow through on my things either," he said.

As we were leaving I looked at his face. In it I could see his young face, too. It was the face I'd looked at throughout my entire young life. A face that had seen my mother, had been there with me on the day she died. Driving home I was lost in thought. I took a wrong turn toward where we used to live. A wave of sadness hit me then, seeing the old neighborhood—the diner where we went on Sundays, and the park where we took our daughter when she was little. I bit down on my lip until it bled, then turned the car around, and headed for home.

ABSENCES

The summer my father left my mother and moved to California to find himself, my mother rented an apartment in a small Upstate New York town called Rome, where she was born, and where her sister and her mother still lived. She wanted us to be closer to people who could help with us as she got back on her feet. She took a job as a waitress at an Italian restaurant on Dominick Street and worked very long and very late nights. After work, she'd come home and soak in a steaming bath, then go into her room and lock the door and cry until the gray hours of morning. We'd sleep late, often until one o'clock in the afternoon, right around the time when *Days of Our Lives* would start, then we'd sit around the kitchen table and stare at the little black-and-white TV on the counter while we ate Cap'n Crunch and my mother smoked cigarettes and drank black coffee. This was classic *Days of Our Lives*; *Days of Our Lives* that had never been better. It was the summer Hope almost married Larry Welch, when Bo, wearing a black leather vest, drove in on his motorcycle to Bonnie Tyler's "Holding Out for a Hero" and rescued her from the wedding. We all stood and cheered and hugged as

Bo drove Hope away on the back of his motorcycle in her giant white wedding gown. There was no one in the world we loved more than Bo.

I didn't understand what it meant that my father had to find himself. To me he seemed to be right there. I didn't know why he left us. My sister and I were good kids and we got along with each other. We didn't cut class or get into fights at school. Our grades were good and our teachers liked us very much. My mother was an excellent cook, she went to church on Sundays, and she kept up her appearance. She was slim, with wavy brown hair, the mom at school all of the boys were in love with.

We didn't hear from my father at all during this time, except for a single picture he sent of himself on a beach in California. In the picture the sky was pink and the low clouds in the distance looked like ghost ships. My father's blond hair was reddish in the setting sun. He was wearing a white T-shirt, faded jeans, sneakers, and sunglasses. My father was a tall, good-looking man—I understood from a young age that he was the kind of man who was hard to hold down: women wanted him, they went after him, and they didn't care about my mother, or about us—and here in this picture, he could have been a movie star. The beach around him was empty; there was not a soul to be seen. I thought of him there alone, then considered that someone else had taken the picture. We hung it on our refrigerator anyway. On the back he wrote the words, just, "Wish you were here." My sister and I were baffled by this sentiment and it took on an enduring importance in our young hearts. Did he mean he wished we, my sister and I, were there, or did he mean my mother? And if he did mean my mother, did that mean he still loved her, that one day he might come back for her and take us all away from this dreary town to a life that was sunny and warm and bright.

That fall I was starting the sixth grade. I hated my new school and all the dumb, dirty-haired kids who went there. My best and only friend was a girl named Julie, a chubby girl who had frizzy red hair, big green eyes, and freckles. Physically, we were opposites; I was tall and thin with brown hair and brown eyes. No one at school liked Julie at all. She had some kind of seizure disorder, a condition I'd never seen before, or since, and sometimes, right when you were in the middle of talking to her, she'd slip into one of her spells. Her eyes would roll into the back of her head and the muscles in her face would freeze and twitch, then, seconds later, just like that, she'd pick up with whatever she was saying as if nothing had happened. Sometimes this would happen over and over while you spoke with her. She said the little seizures were called "absences." She had no memory of them, and while she wasn't exactly sure what triggered them, she assured us that it was absolutely no big deal at all and that we should just ignore it when it happened.

The other kids at school seemed to like me well enough, but this was not the case for Julie. They were not exactly nice to her to her face, but behind her back they were downright vicious: they called her *Beef Jerky* and did hideous impressions of her as she passed them in the hallways, often making each other fall to the floor with laughter. If she knew about this, she never said anything, and she didn't seem to care. She had been held back in second grade and she'd started school a year late, so she was older than everybody else by a mile. She'd already turned thirteen. She already had her period and had boobs and wore a bra. She'd already been as far as third base with her boyfriend, who was sixteen, and who owned his own car, which he picked her up in every day from school. She smoked Marlboro Reds, had tried pot, and even had her own favorite drink, Southern Comfort and lemonade, which we drank at her house some Friday nights when her mother was at work.

On the way to school she liked to stop at Midnight Pharmacy, a small everything store right next to our school. It was owned by a very old man named Mitch whose back was hunched at an unnatural angle. He wore a white button-up shirt, a black tie, and thick glasses. He stood at the cash register doing crossword puzzles and never looked up unless someone came and stood right in front of him. Julie would get to the playground wild with excitement and we'd run to the school bathroom and she'd show me all the things she stole that day, always giving me the things that I wanted most. I'd put on the black eyeliner, rub the strawberry lotion over my arms. "Come with me next time," she'd say, laughing. "It's so fun. You have to try it."

I'd been taught that it was a sin to steal, but I met her there one morning before school anyway. I was afraid we might see a teacher, or someone else from school, but we didn't. We went into the makeup aisle and pretended to be talking about an assignment. I picked up a lipstick, examined it closely, then let it go up the sleeve of my white winter coat as I reached for another. The second one I made an elaborate show of putting back. After that, I slid a black eyeliner into my pocket. My heart pounded and blood rushed to my head. We walked out slowly, still talking about our schoolwork, then we hugged with happiness and ran all the way back to the playground. Before long, we were bringing our backpacks to Midnight Pharmacy, tossing in all the little things that we loved, mostly beauty products and candy. Then we moved on to Great American, a grocery store just down the block from the school, and to the 7-Eleven on the corner of James and Sycamore. It went on for months. I kept the stuff we took at my house—no one went into my room or looked at my things.

My mother was still working late nights at the restaurant, but now she'd made friends with a few of the other waitresses, and after work they'd all go out for drinks. I was usually still awake when she got home. I'd hear her coming in, her body knocking into the table and chairs, glass bottles clanking in the refrigerator, then the click of her lighter, the smell of cigarette smoke, and she'd make her way into her room and fall onto her bed. Only an hour or so before her next shift would she rise to take her shower. I'd stand in the doorway of the bathroom and quietly watch as she put on her makeup. She'd suck her cheeks in to get her reddish blush just right. She'd use a brown pencil to darken her eyebrows, then heat the tip of a black pencil with a lighter and line the top and the bottom of her lid, turning the streak upward at the end to make her eyes look like a cat's. She'd wear red lipstick, always blotting some onto a tissue that she'd leave on the sink, and which I'd see every time I used the bathroom for the rest of the day until I went to bed.

One morning in January, Julie and I were at Great American before school filling our pockets with tiny bottles of shampoo and mouthwash from the sample aisle. I saw a man coming toward us from the front of the store. I watched as he walked slowly up our aisle, looking carefully at all the items on the shelves. He was a skinny man with thick blond hair, dressed neatly in a tan jacket, jeans, and sneakers. When he came along to where we were standing he looked quickly at us, then kept walking down the aisle. He seemed to be somewhat young. He turned the corner and was out of sight, but a moment later he was back again. This time he stopped in front of us.

"Girls," he said, "do you want to come with me?"

I lost my breath. "For what," I said.

"For all the stuff you've been putting in your pockets," he said plainly. He looked around. No one else was in the aisle. Aside from a few cashiers, the store was mostly empty in the early morning.

Julie took a few steps back and glanced over her shoulder, and for a second I wondered if she might try to make a run for it, but then her skin reddened and she started to cry. I tried to inhale but barely got anything in. I thought of my mother's face, the shame she'd feel when she found out what we'd been doing. She didn't need this, not now, and I felt sure it would be the thing that killed her.

"Here," I said, handing the man a crinkled ten-dollar bill from my pocket. My aunt had given it to me for Christmas. I carried it with me in case we ever got caught. I knew it would not be enough to cover even half of what I'd taken that day alone, but it was all I had. "We were going to pay for it," I said. When he looked at me doubtfully I added, "I swear. We were." Then, "Please," I said.

The man shook his head. He took a few steps away from us. For a moment I thought that everything would be okay. But then he turned and said, "Come on now, girls. Put the stuff back, and follow me." He walked a few feet ahead of us. We looked at each other, emptied our pockets, then followed him down the aisle, and past the row of cashiers at the front of the store. There was a swirling feeling in my head. When he walked through the automatic doors and out of the store, Julie and I both froze. "I'll just have to take you to the station for a bit to fill out some paperwork," he said. His face was expressionless. In the store, a young woman in the check-out line played peekaboo with a baby who was fussing in the front seat of her cart. "My car is right here," he said, walking toward an old maroon sedan. He unlocked it. When we didn't move, his tone deepened. "Come on now, girls," he said. "You don't want to make a scene for all your little friends to see." Julie's face was wet with tears now. When we started moving toward the car, the man said very softly, "Good. That's good girls."

I got in behind the driver's seat, and Julie got in behind the passenger seat. I knew she must have been thinking of her mother, a woman who was prone to fits of rage. She'd scream at the top of her lungs sometimes, the slightest things setting her off. I saw her punch through a wall once. Another time, when Julie forgot to empty the dishwasher, she whipped a glass across the room. It hit the wall just behind where Julie was standing, and shattered, and then it was Julie who had to clean it up.

The car smelled of vanilla air freshener and cigarettes. A crystal prism hanging from the rearview mirror shot tiny rainbows everywhere; they flickered and shimmered on the wood paneling of the dashboard. The leather seats were torn in places, the crusted foam leaking through. The engine was loud when he turned the key. Ice-cold air blasted from the heater. The man lit up a cigarette and unrolled the window a crack before pulling away. The sharp air from outside sent chills through my spine as his smoke blew into my face. "I saw what you girls were doing," the man said after a few moments. "Not just today," he said. "I've been watching you for a while."

"What do you mean," Julie said. "This was the first—"

The car was stopped at a red light a few blocks from where I lived. Flurries of snow sat almost motionless in the air. The man turned and looked at us. His eyes were light blue with flickers of darker blue. "Don't lie to me," he said. "Lie to your mommies all you want," he said. "But please don't lie to me." He turned and looked out at the road.

Joey Russo's grandfather was crossing the street with his shopping cart full. When he got safely to the other side the man started driving again. Out the window kids were heading toward the school. There'd been a heavy snowfall the night before, and all morning we had the radio on praying they would announce a snow day. It was good packing snow, and some kids were having snowball fights as they made their way down James Street toward the school. In a few minutes, the bell would ring, and everyone would pour inside, change their wet boots to sneakers, go to their seats, say the pledge, and start their day.

"You girls have to learn that you can't just take things that don't belong to you," the man said.

We drove along Black River Boulevard until it hit Mohawk Drive, then turned on Mohawk Drive, past the air force base and the row of abandoned factories, and a few minutes later, took the exit for Route

49. The car was big, and Julie seemed small and far away on her side
of the back seat. She rubbed her finger along the stiff edge of a rip in
the leather.

"Where are you taking us?" she said.

I reached for her hand and squeezed hard.

The man didn't respond. Instead he started talking about how he
read that it was going to stay cold for a very long time this year. He
said that one year, when he was very young, it snowed all the way
through to the end of May. He went on about his childhood for a
while, his life with his grandmother and his younger brother. He said
there was nothing in the world he would want more than to be back
there with them again.

I looked out the window and kept silent as he talked.

After a moment, he said, "How old are you girls, anyway?" He
made eye contact with me through the rearview mirror. "Aren't you
a little young to be shoplifting?" he said.

"Twelve," I said, though I was still eleven.

"Thirteen," Julie said.

He shook his head, looking disappointed, then lowered his
voice. "You're very beautiful girls," he said gently. He was looking
at me again in the rearview mirror. I felt the skin on my face burn
under his stare. I kept my head turned away. After a while he added, "I
can see that you're smart too." He was quiet for a moment, then
he said, "That's what matters. Your beauty will fade someday when
you're older and all that will be left is what's up here." He tapped his
head. He checked for cars before pulling away from a red light. "You
girls can do great things with your life," he said. "You can do anything
you want to do."

I felt a peace come over me. I liked him very much. I started to
imagine that maybe we could keep in touch after all this was over.
Maybe he could be like a big brother, or an uncle who comes over on

Sundays for dinner. I thought my mother would probably like him too. I caught his eye in the rearview mirror and smiled and he smiled back at me.

Julie was still crying. "It's okay," I said to her. "Don't worry," I said.

"You're not bad girls," the man went on, looking out at the road. "You've just done a bad thing," he said. "There's a big difference there," he said. "It's a very important distinction."

I felt a wave of shame for what Julie and I had been doing, and I promised myself I was done with all that, that I wouldn't take things that didn't belong to me anymore.

Julie started to breathe harder.

"Come on," I said. "Calm down," I told her. "It's going to be okay." The man looked pleased. I went on. "He just has to take us to the station to fill out some paperwork."

The busy road had given way to the country road. I looked out the window and saw barns go by. I'd never been on this road, or anywhere near here. We were getting far from town, far from everything that was familiar. I wondered, then, why he wasn't wearing a uniform. Why he didn't have a police car.

"Hey," I said softly. "Are you really a cop?"

"That's a good question," he said, sort of smiling. His face reddened and he looked around. He lit a cigarette. His forehead twitched. "What else would I be?" he said.

His blond hair was thick and chopped-looking. He had cut it himself. Staring into it, I suddenly felt very dizzy.

"I want to get out of this car," Julie said then. "Let me out of this car," she said.

The man stayed calm. "That's not what's going to happen," he said.

The snow was coming down hard now, just pouring out of the sky, being dumped out of the sky, and all along the road in front of us, in the car, everywhere, the bright whiteness was a blur. I put my head into my knees, pushed against the pulling. I felt as if I might be sucked out of the car and into the sky.

I caught Julie's green eyes and held on. She was breathless now, sweating. She tried the door but it wouldn't open. "Mom," she started to say. "Mom," she screamed. "Mommy." The sound poured into me, filled the car, echoed out into the snow-covered fields all around us.

My heart pounded.

Julie slipped down in her seat, then, and her body became rigid. She started to jerk and twitch. When we first became friends, her mother had warned me that she might have a seizure like this one day. She'd told me what to do to keep her from hurting herself. She said it would last only a few minutes, and that Julie might be a little confused and weak afterward, but she'd be okay. I pulled her head onto my lap, turned her sideways so she wouldn't swallow her tongue.

The man kept glancing at us through the rearview mirror. "What the fuck," he said. "What the fuck is going on," he said. "What's wrong with her," he said, screeching his car to the side of the road. He turned and looked at me, his lips curled with disgust. "Is she some kind of retard," he said. "Is she some kind of fucking freak."

"She's having a seizure," I said.

What happened next happened very fast. He got out of the car and went around to Julie's side. He opened the back door, yanked her out of the car, and let her fall, still convulsing, into the snowbank on the side of the road. I was still. My legs were heavy. I looked up at him and for a second I thought that he would slam the door shut and drive off with me. Instead his face scrunched with anger. "You too," he said. "Get the fuck out," he said through closed teeth. "Get out of my fucking car right now, you freaks." He grabbed my arm and yanked me from the back seat. I stumbled onto the ground next to Julie. He got back in the car and drove away. I pulled Julie's rigid body far away from the road. We had been taken. But now we were free.

A man had us. But now he let us go. A surprising feeling passed over me, then, almost like sadness: he didn't want us. It was a quick, sickening impulse, and I recognized it as strange as soon as I felt it. I turned and vomited into the cold white snow. When I was finally done, Julie's body had softened.

We were far from anywhere, all around us just snowy fields. The cold air stung my face, my hands. I worried about frostbite, amputation. When Julie got enough strength back, we started walking. Just about a half hour down the road was a house. The woman inside was kind. We told her we were lost, and she let us use her phone and her bathroom.

When Julie's boyfriend got there a little while later, he wanted us to call the police and report the man who he was sure would have raped and killed us, but we reminded him that we'd been stealing, committing a crime, and we all agreed that the man would probably go free, if they ever found him at all, while the two of us ended up in juvie. We all promised to never tell anyone about it, and we never did, not even our mothers.

I got a trash bag, a big one, a lawn bag, and filled it with every single thing we ever stole and threw it in the dumpster behind the school. Julie and her boyfriend broke up not long after that, and in junior high, I got in with another crowd, girls who were on the cheerleading squad, who read books for fun and worked on the school newspaper. Before I knew it, Julie and I had completely lost touch. When we'd see each other in the hallways we'd say hi, but that was all. You would have thought that what we'd been through together would have brought us closer, that we'd share some special and unbreakable bond, but it was the opposite: in my mind the whole thing was so intricately connected to her that even a glimpse of her green eyes in the hallway could make me get physically sick.

My father eventually found himself. He came back to New York just over a year after he left looking tan and gorgeous. His hair had turned blond from the sun. He'd had a girlfriend in California, but it didn't work out, and somehow that experience, him having and losing this other woman, made him realize that it was us he'd loved and wanted the whole time, and he didn't want to miss out on any more of our growing up. That was all well and good, except for the fact that he was too late. My mother had a boyfriend now—they were thinking of moving in together—and whatever love she'd held in her heart for him all those nights crying in her room had hardened into something that was more like hate. I didn't blame her: I hated him too. He'd left us for dead. Some absences you can't make up for, and more often than not, walking away from love means walking back to hate. There's nothing you can do about that, except to move on, and try to do better the next time. Or the time after that.

THE HEXTER GIRLS

The Hexter girls lived in a two-family home on the second floor. They had a little top porch that overlooked a busy street. Sometimes they'd curl up out there with blankets on cool nights, and their mother, who was much older than everyone else's mother, would sit in a red-and-blue metal lawn chair and tell them stories about when she was a little girl. They liked to fall asleep listening to her, hearing the traffic noises below. Their mother was a big round woman, and she had a deep warm voice. She was a born-again Christian, and they were too, they supposed. Their mother was always going to church. She went to church three days a week, and had a prayer group with some sisters from the church on the other days. The girls were home alone quite a lot.

Two doors down from where they lived was Rogowski's Funeral Home, a hideous tan brick building covered with dead vines that took up half the block. There was always a wake going on—sometimes there were two wakes in one day, one that began at eleven o'clock in the morning, and one that began at four o'clock in the afternoon. Each time the girls made sure to be out on their top porch. The people going to the wakes parked in front of their house and along their street. The girls liked to watch the people get out of their cars, all dressed up and fancy. The people looked rich. The girls were not rich, and they knew this acutely. At school, other kids called them dirty girls, and said they smelled like pee. They had no friends, but that was okay because they had each other.

One of the girls used money she got from their aunt at Christmas to buy two water guns at Cities, a little convenience store just around the corner from where they lived, and on weekends, the girls draped large towels over the porch banisters and sprayed the people as they made their way to the funeral home with their water guns. When the people were sprayed, they always looked around, and looked up, and they always said, "What in the hell?" Or, "What was that?" Or, "I think a bird just pissed on me." Or, "It must be raining." Or, "It's starting to rain!" Any of which would make the girls fall on their backs with laughter, and they'd hug with laughter, and then they'd get back up and try again to hit someone else.

One day, just before four o'clock, just before the four-o'clock wake, the girls went out onto the top porch with their water guns completely full and sprayed through a little crack between the towels. They'd had a good go of it that morning, had hit a lot of people, and had laughed quite a lot, and they were very excited for the afternoon crowd. But that day, a woman, dressed all in black, looked up, and instead of being baffled, instead of being confused, she looked right at the little girls, and she called up to them.

She said, "I see you up there." Then she said, "Do you think I can't see you?"

The girls' hearts pounded and the blood went away from their faces. They peeked through their little peeking cracks in the towels.

The woman said, "Aren't you the Hexter girls?"

And then with this, the girls felt that they might almost die.

"Stand up," the woman said. "I can see you," she said, "so you might as well just stand up."

The girls stood up. They looked at each other, and they looked at the woman and saw that it was Ms. Davies, the librarian from the school, who could be very mean, and whom they did not like very much. She had scolded the younger girl for not finishing a book in a week, and for wanting to check it out again; she'd told her that a book like the one the girl was reading should take just one hour to read. That's how crazy she was: the book was two hundred pages long.

"That's right," she said now. "I knew you lived here." She was moving her head, trying to look past the girls, into their apartment. "Where is your mother?" she asked. "Are you two up there all alone?" she asked.

The girls nodded their heads.

"Come down here," she said. "Come down here right now," she said. "I'd like to talk to you for a minute," she said. "You can leave your water guns up there."

Again the girls looked at each other. They did not know what to do. Their mother always told them not to let anyone in—but this wasn't that, not quite. Slowly they opened the screen door and went down the stairs. Now they were standing just in front of Ms. Davies. Her dress was very fancy, silky, and she had pearls on, and she looked quite lovely, not at all like how she looked at school. In the second grade, she'd read *Charlotte's Web* to their class, and she cried at the end when they cried—and they'd loved her very much, then.

"That's better," she said, softly. "I remember you girls," she said. "Where's your mother?" she said. "Is she at church?" she said.

"Yes," said one of the girls.

And the other girl said, "We're sorry. We didn't mean to—"

"That's okay," Ms. Davies said. "Come with me," she said. "I want you to meet someone."

She started to walk, and the girls didn't know what to do, so they followed her. When they got to the big doors of the funeral home, one of the girls said, "We can't go in there." They looked down at their clothing. They were dressed in the rags that they wore around the house, and they knew their mother wouldn't want anyone to see them like that. Ms. Davies said not to worry, that it was okay. She patted their backs and walked in behind them. She said it would just be for a minute.

Inside, they walked through long hallways, lit dimly with fancy chandeliers, and lined with dried flowers in tall vases, and dark floral wallpaper. It smelled like a library, old and musty. In one small room, there were rows of pews like in a church all facing an altar. It looked very much like a church, but warmer, and there was a giant oriental rug on the floor, and elegant drapes on the windows. There were not many people in the room at all yet. Just a few. And Ms. Davies took the girls' hands and walked them to the very front of the room.

There, in a wooden box, was a body, a young man's body. He couldn't have been twenty years old. He wore makeup: cover-up, blush, and some sort of lip tint, the girls could tell; his skin looked completely smooth, as smooth as a raw chicken breast. The girls had never seen anything like this before, except in the movies.

"This is my son," Ms. Davies said.

And the girls felt a feeling of horror inside their hearts.

She said again, "This is my son. My boy."

The girls looked again at the man who was handsome with blond hair and a little mustache.

"He had an accident," she said. "Someone was not careful with him and he had an accident."

The girls ran out of the funeral home and back to their house, and many years went by, and the girls were much older, and their mother died, and their husbands left, and their kids had grown, and moved away, and they saw Ms. Davies again, and she was very very old, and they hugged her fiercely then, and they cried, and they told her that they were very sorry for her loss.

Sam's House

We were twenty and Chloe was pregnant. We'd been staying with her aunt, but with the baby coming, it was time to find a place of our own. I saw the ad in the *Observer Dispatch*—beautiful two-bedroom house on a quiet, tree-lined street in New York Mills—and called the number right away. Sam, the owner of the house, kept me on the phone for a while before he let us come to see the place. He asked a lot of questions, said he rented only to people with "character." He'd lived in the house with his wife for many years, he told me, but after she died he bought a condo near the New Hartford Shopping Center. He'd rented it out to a Bosnian couple last year, but now they were retiring to Florida and he was looking for someone to take over.

"A real house," Chloe said. "Imagine that." Growing up, we'd both always lived in apartments. "For four hundred dollars a month," she said. She took a ponytail holder from her wrist, pulled her dark hair into a bun, and curled up beside me on the couch.

"Don't get excited," I told her. "It's probably a crack house," I said. "Apartments in West Utica are going for more than that."

She agreed that it was most likely a waste of time but insisted we look anyway.

When we got there, we were surprised to see that it was nice. A brown cottage at the end of the street with hardwood floors and newer appliances in the kitchen. In the living room there was a sliding-glass door that opened to a large and well-kept yard. Sam walked us around showing us all the rooms. He wore a stained jean shirt and jeans, and had his long gray hair pulled into a low braid at the back of his neck.

"I don't normally ask," he said after he was done showing us around, "but how old are you guys, anyway?" he said. "You look, like, really young." He had a nervous habit of giggling after everything he said.

"We're both twenty," I said, showing him my license. Chloe and I had known each other since the eighth grade, but we'd been seeing each other for only about a year.

Sam took a peek and nodded his head. "It's a good house," he said to us. He cleared his throat. "It has a nice flow," he said. "I think you guys would be very happy here."

We told him that we wanted it and said we'd have him over once everything was settled. Chloe's aunt had lent us the money for the security deposit. I wrote Sam a check for eight hundred dollars, and we moved in a few weeks later. Chloe took her time decorating, picking the colors she wanted to paint the rooms. She picked "Middleton Pink" for the baby's nursery and "Pale Powder" for our bedroom. Sam didn't mind if we painted, he said, as long as we put it back to white when it was time for us to move out.

We got an old teak patio set at a garage sale for the backyard, and a grill. It was the first time either of us owned a grill, or had a backyard for that matter. We ate most of our dinners out there that summer—usually cheeseburgers and hot dogs. Some nights Chloe got fancy and made a tomato-and-cucumber salad, or we grilled chicken. A few times, we even tried grilling a pizza. Chloe bought white lights and I strung them up the trunk of the old maple tree. The older couple had left behind some things, including a small outdoor fountain that sounded like a waterfall. We'd sit out there listening to the fountain go after dinner and talk late into the night. The cold dark felt endless and it seemed we were the only two people on earth.

Chloe told me all about her childhood, her mother always moving them around. She told me about her father too, how he had kids with other women while they were married. She said that when they split her mother completely lost it. She'd stand at the kitchen sink for hours, her hands going wrinkly in the dirty water; sometimes she'd fall to the floor, crying. When that happened Chloe and her sister would help her get to bed. My mother had been a cheater too; we had cheating parents in common. I understood what it did to a person to be on the receiving end. When I was fifteen my father followed my mother to the Country Side Motel on Herkimer Road where she met her lover. He saw them together, checked into his own room, and hung himself. That was it for me having parents. But now Chloe and I were together and things felt solid. We'd made better lives for ourselves than those lives we'd started out with.

About a month after we were settled in we followed up on our promise to have Sam over. Now it was Chloe walking him around, showing him the place.

"Wow," he said as he looked at our things. "You guys have nice stuff," he said, with his giggle. He had on the same stained denim clothes we saw him in the last time. His eyes went to our dining room table—oak, with floral carvings. Chloe had found it at a garage sale, and a set of matching ladder-back chairs too. She was a hell of a nego-tiator and had a way of getting people to give her their things for next to nothing. "It didn't look like this when we lived here," Sam said. He looked through the glass doors and out into the backyard. He was silent for a moment. The white lights were on and the fountain was going. I could see that he was pleased to see the place looking so good.

Chloe liked to make a fuss when people came over; she bought a tomato pie and a chocolate cake. But Sam said he only wanted water. We all went outside and sat down. It was a hot afternoon but there was a breeze. Dark clouds swam through the sky like whales; there'd be rain later, thunder, maybe. Sam crossed his legs one way but then changed his mind and crossed them the other. It was quiet for a few moments, then he asked Chloe what she did for a living.

"I'm a preschool teacher," Chloe said. She looked over at him, searching. Chloe felt uneasy around most men, I knew. She avoided male doctors, even male cashiers at the checkout line.

"You don't say," Sam said. He stood for a second and ripped some stray vines from a shrub. "My wife was a teacher," he said. Then, after a moment he added, "Youngins." He laughed and he rubbed at his nose.

Chloe went on. "Someday," she said, "I want to start my own preschool."

I knew from the dealership that whenever someone says *someday* that usually means *never*. I looked away.

"Wow," Sam said. "That's something," he said. "I bet you'd be great at that."

Chloe blushed. She put her hand on her belly, which seemed to have doubled in size since we'd last seen him. "For now, though," she said, "I'm just focusing on this." Her voice softened.

I looked at her, and I could see that she felt me looking at her, but she kept her eyes down. I wondered if this was what she really wanted, and I wondered if she was wondering that too. When we first found out she was pregnant, we had considered ending it; we even scheduled an appointment at the clinic. But then Chloe had a dream of a little girl with ringlets in her hair, and after that she decided she wanted to keep it. She even got excited, started buying tiny clothes.

Sam told us that he lived alone. He was an electrician and kept busy with that. "There's always work," he said. "Sometimes I have to go all the way to Buffalo to get it," he said, laughing. Then he collected himself. "Don't get me wrong," he said. "I'm not complaining." He slid his hand over his braid and drank his water. His eyes moved around the yard.

I guessed he was about as old as my father would have been and I felt sorry for him, living alone. And there was a pang of guilt too: here I was, settled into his house with my living and breathing girlfriend, a baby on the way. It felt somehow as if I'd taken something from him. I had the impulse to apologize, to say something. I wondered how his wife died, why they never had kids. But all of that seemed too personal to ask. After about a half hour, Sam said he had something else to do, and he stood up and shook our hands and left.

Chloe shivered when he closed the door. "That guy gives me the heebie-jeebies," she said. "Something's not right with him," she said. She went into the kitchen and scrubbed her hands. "Let's never do that again."

"He's a sweet guy," I said. I watched him in his pickup truck. He sat out front for a while before pulling away. "Leave him alone," I said.

The first bit of trouble came after Chloe had the baby. It was a bad winter; the snowbanks on the side of the road were waist-high for months. We had no money for a sitter, and no one to help us. I was working at the Honda dealership on Commercial Drive and had to stay late hours. When I'd get home Chloe would be in tears, her sweatshirt stained with milk and the elastic on her pants wearing thin. The baby would be in the other room, red-faced and screaming. "I can't fucking do this," she'd yell. She'd get in the car and drive and I don't know how far she'd get but she'd always be back within a few hours and then she'd be calm. "I'm sorry," she'd say. "I just get so overwhelmed," she'd say.

We didn't see Sam much during this time. The house was in good repair and there was very little that went wrong. He stayed away, gave us our space. Aside from the rent check I sent him every month, it felt as if it were our house. He did call one night after Chloe left for one of her drives to say that a neighbor had complained about our fighting. He wanted to know was everything okay. I started to tell him about the baby, and how hard it was, about how long the days were for Chloe with no one to help her, and before I knew it I was in tears.

"I'm sorry," I said. "I'm not like this," I said. "It's just"—I took a moment to swallow it down. "We haven't been getting much sleep lately," I said. When Sam didn't say anything, I added, "We didn't know it'd be this hard."

Sam said it was okay and that he understood. He got off the phone quickly, and if there were any more complaints about our fighting, he didn't call to tell us.

By the time the baby turned six months old, things settled down considerably. The baby was sleeping through the night now, and Chloe was back to her normal self more or less. There was still the extra weight, the stained sweatshirts. But the rage that seemed to consume her in those early months had shifted into something more manageable. Something ordinary.

Then the weather changed and the birds came back from wherever they'd been. Suddenly everything became a sacred moment, a moment we needed a picture of. The baby was making her first sounds. There was her first smile, her first laugh. She was having her first solid food. Her first avocado. Her first sweet potato. Her first chicken soup. Now her first words. The baby was crawling, get the camera, quick. She's taking her first steps. Look, she's dancing. Singing. All this was better than any drug I'd ever done. If you had to ask me if I could go back to any moment in my life, it would be right here to these moments. As I was living them I knew these would be the ones. I wished I could press pause, stop things, or at least find a way to put it in slow motion. I knew nothing else would ever be as good as this.

One Saturday around noon Sam came by with a woman. He usually gave us some notice before stopping by, just a day or two to get things in order, but not this time.

"This is my friend," he said, "Karen." He gestured toward a tall woman in a suit who had shoulder-length blond hair. "Do you mind if we have a look around?"

"Feel free," I said. "It's your house."

The woman smiled without making eye contact. She moved the strap of her purse closer to her neck and walked into the house. Chloe was still in her pajamas. She had been nursing the baby on the couch when they arrived and she kept at it, grabbing a blanket to cover herself. The dryer was going in the bathroom, zippers clanked against metal. I could see Chloe was feeling self-conscious about how she looked, about the dishes in the sink, the laundry on the bathroom floor.

Sam walked Karen from room to room and they said things to each other in hushed voices. They stood in the doorway of the little kitchen and she pointed at the wall, waving her finger around. Sam nodded his head as she spoke, stared out blankly. I didn't like how it felt sitting there having people walking around, looking at our things. But there wasn't much I could do about that.

After a few minutes they both thanked us. Sam laughed his awkward laugh, waved to us from near the front door, and then they left.

"He's going to evict us," Chloe said. "That creep probably realized he could be getting more money."

"He's not going to evict us," I said. Through the blinds I watched them talking in front of the house for a minute. "I don't know what that was," I said. "We're good tenants. We pay the rent. We take care of the place."

Chloe handed me the baby, who'd fallen asleep. She opened her laptop and googled the address. "I bet he's already got it listed," she said. "His friend, my ass," she said. "She's probably going to pay eight hundred dollars a month," she said. "That's how much houses in Whites—"

I saw a change in her eyes as she looked at the screen. Her mouth fell open, and her face went pale. A moment passed.

"What?" I said.

She didn't say anything.

"What," I said, louder. "Tell me."

"Someone was murdered here," she said at last.

Chloe was prone to hysterics and I was used to that, prepared for it, skilled at handling it, but now a stillness fell over her. "His wife," she said.

My heart quickened. I felt the blood go away from my head, and I felt a rush of shame. With all the excitement of Chloe being pregnant, it never occurred to us to look the place up before moving in. I brought the baby to the nursery and set her down in her crib. I looked up the address myself; now I was reading the articles in the *Observer Dispatch* too. There was a fuzzy familiarity to the story; reading it felt like recapturing a dream. Just over two years before we moved in there was a home invasion. The police described it as a burglary gone wrong. Sam had been away for work. His wife was in bed when the burglar came in, and that was where he killed her: blunt force trauma to the head, one article said. He buried her body in a shallow grave in the backyard and took her car. For a week she was reported missing, then their dogs started to dig up the ground, and there she was. They found her car and the guy who did it in Pennsylvania a few weeks after that.

That afternoon a light went out inside of Chloe. She wouldn't talk. In the days that followed she continued to retreat; I could see her moving inside of herself. She was terrified to be in the house without me and would not step foot in the backyard. She'd spend her days at the park, or, if it was raining, she'd go to the mall. She'd pack a lunch for herself and one for the baby. At night she'd crawl into bed beside me after putting the baby down, breathless with panic.

I thought she would have tried to put it behind her, but it was just the opposite. She became obsessed with the story, wanted more. She kept looking it up online, asking neighbors what they knew. She found a letter Sam had written to the judge. In it, he said they'd been childhood sweethearts, that she was the love of his life. In a forum somewhere she found a post from a niece saying she wanted the case opened up; she didn't think they found the right guy. Chloe emailed the niece, and they wrote each other back and forth. She even had lunch with her once. She started looking for other places for us to live, and cropped all the photos as best she could to remove all traces of the house. She became very thin and started smoking again. Months went by like this, her moving further and further away from me. Then one day, I came home from work, and she had packed up all of her things and all of the baby's things. She said she was leaving. "This is a sign," she said. "Women die here," she said.

I didn't believe in signs. Didn't believe the universe took the time to offer up clever hints to us about how we should live our lives. I felt like I might throw up. I didn't understand why we couldn't get past this. I begged her to let it go. I said it didn't matter what happened here before we lived here.

"I'm not in the right place," she said, looking me in the eye. "I don't belong here," she said. She said she loved me, but this was something she had to do for herself. She said she'd made up her mind and I shouldn't try changing it. She was going to move back in with her aunt, start again. She hoped she could figure out a way to go to college, get on with her plan to start a preschool. She said she'd work it out so we could both raise the baby.

I can't say I was surprised at this point; I knew that it was coming. But it was coming so fast and I didn't know how to stop it. When I was younger, and first started driving, a car ran a red light getting onto the Parkway and smashed into the car in front of me. I didn't hit them and there was a moment of relief—I somehow managed to stop in time. But then I looked in my rearview mirror and saw that the car behind me was coming full speed; it was not going to be able to stop in time. This was like that. I sat there waiting for the impact, nowhere to go, nothing to do.

"You're sure this is what you want?" I said.

"Yes," she said. She was crying.

"Once you go, things will be different."

"I know," she said. "I'll be okay. We'll be okay," she said.

It was a long time before I understood that this was just something that happens in life, how people harden on you when you least expect them to, and won't ever go soft again no matter how much you want them to, and how you have no choice but to just accept it, though it's the last thing in the world you want to do. *Come back. Come back,* I wanted to scream. *Please, change back.*

But she did not come back.

I let Sam know we were moving and I painted the walls white again. A few weeks later, after I'd moved our furniture to an apartment three miles away, Sam said he wanted to do a walk-through with me so he could give us our deposit back. On the last day of the month, he came by and we went through the house together. Everything was as he'd left it, nothing was damaged.

"I'm sorry about this," I said to him. "I thought we'd be here longer," I said.

"Hey," he said tenderly. "It's not your fault," he said. He was quiet. "I was actually thinking I might sell it this year anyway," he said. He looked around at the blank walls, the empty rooms. I saw a sadness in him and I felt sad too, seeing the house this way.

"I wanted to say," I said at last, "I'm very sorry about what happened with your wife," I said. "We read about it online."

Sam's eyes locked on mine for a quick second, then he looked away. His face reddened and I thought he might cry. He went to say something, then shrank a bit. A few moments passed. "I guess I should have told you guys," he said.

I shook my head, patted his shoulder. "That had to be hard," I said.

Sam caught my eye and nodded and looked at the floor. He wrote me a check for the security deposit and we both left and that was the last time I saw him.

Many years later, after Chloe and I had both married other people and had other lives, we talked about Sam's house. It was the day our daughter graduated from high school; she was going to be moving to California in a few months for college. Chloe had put on some weight, but her hair was still long and dark, and her eyes were the same. She was wearing a light dress and a long cardigan. She told me her son would be starting high school in the fall. After that there was some small talk and some silence. A group of graduates stood posing for a picture just beyond where we were standing. Her eyes rose to mine. "We weren't much older than that," she said, "when we lived at Sam's house."

I smiled. "You read my mind," I said.

It was a cool day for June, there was a chill in the air. A red bird kept coming back to the tree where we were standing for twigs that had fallen to the ground. We watched the bird for a while.

"How different life turned out to be," she said, "from what we thought it would be."

It wasn't a question or a regret, just something she was thinking at that moment, and her sharing it with me made me feel close to her in a way I never thought we could again. I caught her eye and held it for a minute, and neither of us said anything, then she smiled, and looked at the ground, and walked away.

I thought of those nights at Sam's house, when we'd stay up late in the backyard talking, how after, we'd get into bed and make love as if we'd never done it before. How much I wanted her. I wished I could remember all the things we talked about, but I couldn't. All I could remember was a feeling. *You are loved,* the feeling said. *This is what love is,* it said.

"Someone died here," she'd say when she crawled into bed in those first nights after we found out, her dark eyes scanning the room. "Right here in this bedroom," she'd say.

I was terrified too, though I never said anything. My mind played it over and over again, *blunt force trauma to the head.* "Someone died everywhere," I'd tell her. "Bad things have happened everywhere," I'd say. A reminder that all that separates you from pain and horror is time.

The One Who Keeps the Washcloth Cold

Bobby rode with her in the ambulance. Her first son, from her first marriage, he'd taken her to some of her appointments, and so he knew the doctor. "It could be hours or it could be days," was what the doctor was telling him now after examining her at the hospital.

When he saw her last, two days ago, she looked seven years younger. "Mama," he said when he first got to her house. "Look what I have for you." And what did he have for her? A dumb stuffed lamb. A child's toy. It played "You Are My Sunshine"; its bashful blue eyes and soft fur made him remember the ease of her old smile.

At the hospital, she was buried under white sheets. Something serene in the sound of the heart monitor. It was steady and unchanging and *there, there*. The rest of the family—Bobby's stepfather, Richard, and his two adult sisters, Annie and Jane, arrived. They stayed quiet when they saw her. Sat in metal chairs. Breathed. Bobby told them what the doctor said: how when you die of cancer, you die piece by piece, part by part. Eleanor's kidneys had died already. Her liver too. Waiting for the other parts, she was hooked to an IV from which liquid morphine dripped.

Awake—*yes*—she was awake. "Mama, I—" Asleep—*oh*—asleep again. Minutes. Hours, like this.

They took turns giving Eleanor tiny sips of water when she awakened. Ice chips. Rubbed her lips with wet cotton swabs. Held her cold, limp hands. Didn't know what to do. Looked around. Dim room. Shiny speckled floors. Listened to the dim buzz from the bleak light. Everyone wanted to be the one whose job it was to keep the washcloth on her forehead cold. But that took only one, and it was Bobby.

"What *is* that noise?" a young nurse said as she came into the room. After a while Bobby realized she was talking about Richard, who had fallen asleep.

"Used to it," he told her. "Didn't even notice."

She added something to Eleanor's IV, adjusted her body in the bed. She was down to ninety pounds, but her body had gained a new weight. It was hard to move her and Bobby struggled not to watch as the tiny nurse got her right in the adjustable bed. It was hospital policy, she said, for him not to help. The nurse checked to make sure the tubes were connected as they should be, and when she did this, a bit of Eleanor's stomach showed. Everyone saw. Her stomach was sagging and blackened. But that was not what everyone was looking at. They were looking at the lump that was underneath her skin. It was the size of a grapefruit. And after they looked at it, they looked away. They looked at one another and then they looked down. They closed their eyes. A sliver of skin was left exposed, and just as the nurse made her way out of the room, Bobby rushed to cover it. Not now. Years later. They would talk about it.

After a while Annie and Jane's whispering turned to talking. Richard let his eyes fall to the TV. Annie was telling Jane about her three-year-old son, Aidan. Last week, after she put him to bed, she heard noises from his room. "I opened the door," she said, "and he had colored himself from head to toe with red marker!"

"Hands full with that one," Richard said with a grin.

Bobby sat in the windowsill. The snow was coming down hard. Whirling so that he could not see the cars in the lot. Packing snow, he could tell. It wasn't going anywhere. The roads would be slick straight through the night. His mind went to his wife, Renee, who was at home with their infant son; right now she was probably nursing him to sleep in the rocking chair. Jane had been looking at him, and he lent her this smile.

"You must've let him have it," Jane said.

"Just the opposite," Annie went on. "I *completely* ignored it. I just said, 'Didn't Mommy tell you it's time to go to sleep?' And he just looked at me for a minute and—I swear to God—collapsed and fell right asleep."

Bobby shook his head. He knew *that* feeling. How many times had someone not seen what was written all over his face? Even his own sisters left him feeling this way at times. He didn't know what it was—sometimes he thought maybe it was because they had a different father—there was just some disconnect. His sisters. He loved them. Had spent every day of his young life with them. Would have done just about anything for them. But understand them half of the time? He could not.

He looked outside again at the storm. Imagined himself a still figure in an old-fashioned snow globe. *If only he could make the world stop shaking.* After a moment he said, "Remember when she used to put maple syrup on snow, tell us it was ice cream?"

In the waiting room the couches were long enough for two people to lie down on; Annie and Jane shared one; Bobby had the other. Richard stayed in the room with Eleanor. He did not let go of her hand. He slept in a chair next to her bed, let his head fill the other half of her pillow.

No one knew quite what to do. It was too soon to say I'm sorry, but there was a need for something. Annie and Jane started making the calls. Bobby went to the cafeteria for coffee. As he left he heard them whispering. They were saying they hoped they went fast when it was their time. And not like Eleanor.

Returning with the foam cups, he passed an old man in the hallway, just ten feet from where his sisters were sitting. Bobby gave the cups to his sisters and looked over again to the man, who was dressed nicely enough in a wool coat and tan pants. But something else: bits of hospital gown were peeking out from under his coat. Over his shoulder was a pillowcase filled with things. And no shoes! Annie and Jane must have taken this in too; they were smirking curiously to each other.

Bobby shot a look in their direction. Couldn't they see there was some problem here? But when he caught their eye, saw the beaten-down looks on both of their young faces, he forgave them. This was more than they could handle. Something he understood about himself from when he was very young: he did not fall apart the way other people did.

"Sir, can I help you with that?" Bobby said to the man. "Where are you heading?"

"To my car—to the parking lot," the old man said, looking straight ahead. He started to walk again, but after a few steps lost his breath and had to stop for a rest. His breathing was heavy with deep wheezing sounds. Sweat dripped from his wrinkled forehead, drenched his thin gray hair.

"Sir," Bobby said, walking toward him, "you don't have any shoes on." He added, "There's snow on the ground." He placed his hand under the man's elbow. "I can't let you go out there without your shoes."

The man said, "Don't worry about that. Got my shoes in the car." He said, "My wife's got my shoes." He took another few steps and then stopped again. He gestured toward a wheelchair with his index finger and then tipped his head toward Bobby. "How's about giving me a lift, Sonny?" he said.

Something came over Bobby: his sister's grins, the old man's packed pillowcase. "I'll take you to your wife," he said, and he helped the old man into the wheelchair, and without turning around, he walked off toward the elevator, pushing the chair.

He was careful not to make eye contact with any of the nurses or doctors. He moved fast, and the old man didn't say anything. He hoped people would assume he was the man's son, that he was taking his father home, and wouldn't ask questions. As he walked, he started to think about what would happen when he opened the door. He knew that if no one was there, he would need to bring the old man back inside. It occurred to him how much he was hoping there would be a wife waiting. He hoped there would be someone waiting there, with a smile on her face, ready to take this old man home and out of his hospital gown. He hoped she would have a pair of shoes for the man's bare feet and something sweet and homemade for the man to nibble on during the ride home. He decided he would help the man put his shoes on, and help him get settled into the car too.

When they got to the door Bobby stopped. The old man squirmed, tried to see outside, past the glare. Bobby closed his eyes and started to pray. He knew that when he went back upstairs, it wouldn't be long before he and his sisters went back into the room. They would walk up to Eleanor, one by one, and kiss her as she lay there on the bed. Nothing else to happen between them. She would open her eyes, say goodbye. She would thank them for everything. Talk slow. Unsure what to say back. Hard to look her in the eyes. Say, "You've been a good mother." Say, "I love you, Mama." And when they left to go to their cars later, they would each sit alone and cry before driving off to their separate homes. They would imagine how she would look the next time they'd see her. A stranger will have put makeup on her, and it would not be the same.

"Come on," the man said. "You're not going to stand here all night, are you?"

"No sir," Bobby said, and he opened the door.

REALTOR

When he opened the door to leave, he reached down and grabbed a sheet of paper from her porch.

"Oh look," he said, "my competition." It was an ad another real estate agent had left at her door while he was doing his walk-through inside her house. On the paper were photos of a home that had recently sold in the neighborhood, and the name and contact information for that real estate agent.

She came over to the door. "Is it Adaline Valentine? she said with a laugh. This was the name of a new realtor in the area who'd undertaken particularly aggressive marketing strategies: last month, on the Fourth of July, she'd planted a patriotic pinwheel in the front right corner of every single lawn for sixty blocks of their Los Angeles neighborhood. And just that week she'd rented a donut truck and drove slowly through the streets after dinnertime with a megaphone, shouting from an open window, "Adaline Valentine's got the free donuts."

Now they were both in the doorway laughing. It was just the right thing to say. Adaline Valentine. The only thing sillier than the woman's over-the-top marketing stunts was her ridiculous rhyming name. He was laughing so hard that he allowed his real, high-pitched and slightly feminine laugh to come through. He was usually better at hiding this laugh except when he was at home, or with his buddies from childhood. "You really are very funny," he said, raising his eyebrows and bending toward her. He had already noted how funny she was when they were at her dining room table. She'd made this face when he pulled out the folder with all the information he'd gathered about the house. It was something he brought to all of his walk-throughs—it was an easy way to impress potential clients. He'd collect all the legal forms that were publicly available about the house and put them in a folder in chronological order, that was all. People liked this sort of attention in the same way they thrilled at hearing their own name in conversation. It was such an easy thing to do. It took about fifteen minutes, and then the forms came in handy later when it was time to sell, so there were no surprises with permits or anything else. But the way she winced when he told her what was in the folder made him *giggle*—he'd actually giggled like a schoolgirl. It was as if she thought he'd uncovered something scandalous about her and he was about to reveal it.

He looked down again at the sheet of paper that the other realtor had left at the door. It was August in the valley and brutally hot. He'd taken off his suit jacket and had it resting over his elbow.

She stepped closer to him and put her fingers on the corner of the paper. It was as if an electrical current ran through the paper when her fingers made contact with it, and he felt his heart rate accelerate at her proximity. She was wearing a floral-print sundress with spaghetti straps. Moles and beauty marks decorated her shoulders. He let go of the paper and she took it in her hand, barely glancing at it. "Thank you again for coming by," she said. "It really was helpful and I appreciate it."

She was going to be selling the little house where she'd once lived with her ex-husband, and she wanted to know which improvements she should make to yield the biggest return on her investment. He'd told her some things she could do to interest potential buyers. He said to spend any extra money she had on the kitchen—a kitchen sells a home—and to do whatever she could to enhance the front landscaping. People make up their minds very quickly when buying a house, usually within the first fifteen seconds of opening the door. But her house was cute; he was sure he'd have no trouble getting lots of offers over asking for her when the time came.

"Of course," he said, looking down. He stepped out onto her porch but then quickly took a step back in and grabbed the paper between his thumb and index finger again, so that they were both holding it. "Which one did she show?" he said. He mumbled the address that was listed on the paper, "11622 Lindley Ave.," he said softly. He scanned the images of the home's interior. He was genuinely interested to see which house it was. It always killed him when anyone in this neighborhood went with another agent.

They both stood there holding one side of the paper, staring down at it. They were standing very close, half facing each other. Neither one of them moved or said anything. There was no noise outside for a while, then the rattle of a gate, and the sound of her neighbor dragging his garbage bin up the driveway. They both looked at the paper. A moment passed. Then another. And another. Now, something was happening, and it was too late to act like it wasn't. She didn't know what to do. And neither did he. He had a very strong feeling, then, that when he left, he was going to miss her terribly, unbearably, even, as soon as he got into his car. After what felt like a very long time he let out a sigh.

"Okay," he said.

"Okay," she said.

"I guess I'll go now," he said, moving not at all. He looked at his car parked in front of her house and felt momentarily lifted. It was important for a realtor to drive a very nice car, especially in Los Angeles. It was important to make a very good first impression. Everything in real estate, and in life, he supposed, was about making a very good first impression. This was harder for him when he was younger and first starting out, but not so much anymore. He was the top realtor at his agency, the top 1 percent of all realtors in the country. When the lease on his Toyota expired a year ago, he decided to lease a Porsche. As a little boy in Upstate New York he never would have even dreamed of having a car like this. His mother did not have her own car, and his father, when he emerged, drove an old Chevy pickup truck. Now he was always careful to park his car right out in front of any house he went in so that he could see it from all the front windows as he walked through the house. The car soothed him. Catching a glimpse of it outside was like hearing his mama's voice. One look at it through the window was like hearing her tell him that everything was okay. *Your life is okay, baby boy,* the car called out to him. *You've made it,* she was saying.

They were both still holding on to the paper.

And what did she want? The only thing? Someone real. Someone who could sit with her and cry at night and tell her about his life, the whole stupid thing, and say the words that went through her own mind lately, when she thought about her own life: it's all been so damn hard. She'd let him cry. She'd let him weep if he wanted to; she could take it—it didn't bother her to see a man this way. She'd hold him, tell him that it was going to be okay now.

"You don't have to be so brave," she heard herself say. She was not looking at him.

"I don't?" he said, sort of laughing.

"Or strong all the time," she said.

"Not me? Not really?" he said, laughing a little again.

They were both still holding the paper.

"I thought that I did," he said. "I thought that I had to." Now he was looking at the ground. He thought she must have been kidding, but he couldn't be sure.

He was older than her. Ten years maybe, she guessed. Fifteen maybe. She couldn't tell. Not much older. Not too, too much older. But enough that it would have felt nice to sit down in front of him, and let him brush her hair. He was probably about fifty.

It was quiet. She said again, "Well, anyway, it really was so nice meeting you." It had been. In the hour or so that he'd been there to talk about her house, they kept slipping into these intimate conversations, about her daughter (who was turning out to be surprisingly mean for her young age), her mother (who had recently passed away), and both of their plans to move away someday (anywhere but Los Angeles, please God). She found herself having to keep reminding herself that she was not with a dear friend, and embarrassed that she kept going on the way she was with a complete stranger.

After another moment, he said, "This is going to sound weird, but I keep having this strange feeling that I'm going to miss you when I get in my car."

"It doesn't sound weird," she said softly. "I feel like I'm going to miss you too," she said.

"What is this?" he said. "Something is happening."

"I think that it is."

"It's very strong."

"I know." She felt homesick for him. Could you miss someone you'd only just met an hour ago who had not even left yet? She guessed you could. She was going to miss him. She was going to die of missing him, she knew, the second he was gone.

Finally she said, "If you wanted to come back in, that would be okay with me."

"It would?" he said. "I can come back in?"

There was that little tone again. It was so soft. So gentle and unsure. It broke her heart coming from a man his age in such a fancy suit like the one he was wearing. A man who had feathered his hair so carefully to cover up the thin spots. She'd heard it earlier when they were going through his three-ring binders at the dining room table. In the first binder, he was telling her about staging a home, and how you get 600 percent back on your investment for every dollar you spend. "People are buying a lifestyle," he'd told her, "not a house. You need to show them how their life is going to be different, how it's going to be better." He'd shown her before and after pictures of some of the houses he'd recently sold, how he'd staged them, and the changes he had made so that they'd sell for more. In one picture, he'd had the old wooden bathroom cabinets painted mouse gray. In another, he'd had the yellow living room walls painted crisp white. He'd brought in designer patio furniture for the photo shoots, faux-fur blankets and outdoor firepits. It was then that he brought out a half-inch binder with laminated client testimonials inside. His voice became very, very gentle when he told her about the letters. "These are letters my clients wrote about me," he said. "They mean everything to me." And when he handed her the folder, she noticed that his hands were trembling.

Now, in the doorway, his voice was very delicate like this again. "Yes," she said. "I'd like it if you came back in," she said. She walked inside and almost sat back down at the dining room table where they'd been sitting before, but instead she sat down on the floor just next to the table. "Come over here," she said. He was still in the doorway. "Right here," she said, and she patted the floor beside her. "I want you to sit down right here with me and tell me all about it."

He glanced at his car one last time, sadly. He felt his life was about to change, felt the weight of a long-overdue goodbye. The sun rolled over the hood of his car and made the paint twinkle like little stars. He took a breath and closed his eyes. He walked over to her and sat on the floor beside her quietly. She looked at him, and he put his head on her lap. He understood this would be okay with her, that she would like it.

"It's been so hard," he found himself saying. He felt as if he was going to cry. "It has all been so hard." And then he did start to cry a little bit.

"Oh," she said. "It's okay," she said. "Don't cry."

He reached up and touched her short, dark hair.

And then she said, "Or, if you want to cry, that's okay. You can cry if you want to. You can let it out."

"I never know who I'm going to meet when I'm at the door. I never know what's going to be inside," he said. "Sometimes it's a beautiful house, and that's great, because then I know I'm going to make a lot of money." He looked at her. "But it's so scary," he said. "I have to go into people's homes and perform. I have to sell myself."

"Oh, but everyone likes you," she said.

"Maybe now," he said. "But they didn't used to. They didn't always like me. And that was very, very hard."

"Oh, come on," she said. "Look at that face. I'm sure they always liked you."

"I didn't always look like this," he said, covering his face with both of his hands. "I used to be ugly. I was like an ugly little house. I realized if I wanted to be successful—like, really successful—I had to do something about it."

"No," she said, peeling his hands away from his face. "But you're so handsome."

"I had all these surgeries," he said. He ran his fingertips over a scar just behind his ear. "No one wants to hire an ugly realtor. Did you know the house actually sells for more if the realtor is attractive?"

"Show me," she said, touching his cheek with her fingers. Now that she was looking, she could see the faint lines of scars under the stubble of his graying beard. "What did they do to you?" she said.

He turned so that he was on his side, and one by one he started to show her the scars. On the side of his face, all along his ear, was a jagged line from his facelift. Then, just below that, on his neck, behind the bottom of his earlobe, there was a one-and-a-half-inch vertical line. The scar was deep, and you could see it easily. She was surprised she hadn't noticed it right off. She ran her finger along it, and when she did, he closed his eyes and winced as if it hurt. "What is this?" she said, rubbing it gently. "What happened to you here?"

"A few things," he said, caressing his neck gently with all of his fingers. "First they did a neck lift," he said. "They sucked out all the fat and tightened the muscles. Once that healed, they added a jaw implant," he said, running his index finger over the line of his jaw. She caught his eye, and he looked deeply sad. "I really needed it," he said. "It completely changed how I look. From the side I used to look like a tur—"

"And this?" she said, touching his chin. There was a short, vertical white line.

"A chin implant."

"And your eyes?" she said.

"I had them lifted."

"And your cheeks."

"Just Botox and fillers," he said. "Oh, and some very small implants," he added with a hint of pride.

She pulled back, took in his whole face. Tried to imagine him as he was without the parts. "Is there anything else?" she said.

He rubbed at his nose. "Isn't that enough?" he said.

"You didn't have to do all this," she said. She felt very sad for him, wondered what he really looked like, and what it must feel like not to look like who you are. "Why did you do this?" she said. "How many surgeries have you had?"

He started to cry. "I honestly don't know," he said. "A lot. So many. And it was so hard. And I look so weird now. Do you think that I look weird?"

"You poor, wounded creature," she said. "Who let you do this? Who told you this was okay?"

"You wouldn't have liked me before. You wouldn't have even given me the time of day," he said.

She thought of earlier, at the table, when he got to the binder about himself with the client testimonials. In it he had a chart, a literal bar graph with his name, and the names of all the other local realtors, and his bar, the blue one, was at least five times as long as the next longest bar. That was how much he'd outperformed his competition. And then he came closer to her, he'd changed chairs so that he was sitting not across from her, but beside her, and when he did, she noticed his hands trembling, and she heard that gentleness in his voice, and she understood he was nervous. She could see the boy then, in him, chubby and unsure. Maybe he'd lost his mother too young, or maybe his mother never had enough time for him to start with. Something. She could see the raw, unmasked soul right there at her kitchen table. How sweet and rare to see a person like this. To see a person at all. People usually did a much better job at hiding themselves.

"I liked your voice," she said. "Whatever you would have looked like, I would have liked your voice," she said. "But you're here now. I've found you now."

He nodded his head and smiled faintly. Then he said, "I never feel like myself anymore."

She walked him over to a large mirror on the other side of the room and stood beside him. She said, "Look at you. You're a beautiful man. Look how tall you are. Look how big your chest is. Look how sturdy you are. Do you think there isn't a woman out there who wouldn't love to curl up in those arms?" She stood in front of him in the mirror. She looked tiny next to him in her sundress.

He put his arms over her, and she smiled.

When he looked at himself there in that moment, he had to say he did feel handsome. Even after all the surgeries, he'd never thought of himself in that way.

"You never had to be perfect, or all those other things. Will you just look at yourself?" she said. "Really just look."

He looked in the mirror. The way they'd branded men his size as "big and tall," they may as well have called them "big and dumb" or just "big dumb oafs." He'd had to shop at separate stores from when he was a teen; it was a source of shame. But seeing the delicate and lovely way she was leaning in to him now made him feel different about the space he occupied in the world. At once he felt strong and powerful and—to use her word, why not, it was just the right word—sturdy. He wanted to lift her up in the air and swing her around, to show her how wonderful she was making him feel, and he knew that he could physically do it, he just wasn't certain if it would be what she'd like, so instead he said, "Why are you doing all this for me?"

"Not *for* you," she said, tipping her head as they both looked at their reflections. "I'm *with* you now."

All night those words ran through his head over and over and over again. While they were talking and then making love and then talking and then making love again, and falling asleep, and even after, when she had fallen asleep, and he was lying there awake staring at her while she was silent and naked and beautiful. He heard those words: "I'm with you now," and for the first time in his life he didn't feel alone.

In the months that followed she drove him back to the plastic surgeon and she made the plastic surgeon remove all the implants that he'd put in, one by one. This required several long and very complex and difficult surgeries. She instructed the doctor to remake the old neck and jaw exactly as it had been with fat taken from his abdomen, complete with the exact same slope that went directly from his bottom lip straight to his Adam's apple with no angles or sharp interruptions to the flow. She fed him foods that were high in omega-3 fatty acids so that he could healthfully get back to what was his naturally comfortable size. It was necessary to undertake this process quite slowly to give his skin the time it needed to gradually stretch back out. When the lease on his Porche finally expired, she went with him to get a Toyota. He started to feel like himself again. His old self. And he looked okay, he really did. He was not so bad. They moved to Santa Barbara, which was not very far from Los Angeles, but far enough away that it felt very different, yet still close enough that he could get back easily to do business with his most prominent clients whenever they needed him. Following the move, her daughter subsequently became less mean, and they were very, very happy together. It was the happiest time in both of their lives. And when he thought back on that person he had temporarily become, he felt very bad that he had let that happen to himself, and unsure about how he'd ever gotten so lost.

But there was one thing that he had not told her about. He'd kept a secret. At the time he kept it, it felt as if it were just a very small secret, a secret that was okay for him to keep for himself, but as time went by, it started to feel bigger. The nose on his face was not his real nose. He'd been born with a different nose. His real nose was like his mother's nose had been: absolutely sickening. It came down in an almost perfect hook that nearly touched his top lip. It took the doctors three surgeries to file it down to a normal size. He did not believe she could ever have loved him with a nose like the one he was born with, and he was certain that if he had told her about it all that time ago on the floor beside her kitchen table, or at any other point in their relationship, she would have made the doctors build it back onto his face, and then she would not have been able to love him, and she would have left. He'd despised the thing all of his life. He'd hated himself when he had it. He did not want to go back to having it. He did not believe she could love him with it, and he wanted to spare her from having to try, and so he decided to carry out this one little lie of omission, and keep this one little secret.

But every time he saw her eyes fall softy on his face, and on his chin and even on his jaw, he started to wonder how nice it might feel if she were looking at him with all that love and seeing his real nose too. Maybe she didn't *really* love him at all. Maybe it was just something about this artificial nose, and the way it worked together with these other features; maybe there was something delightful in this false combination. But it wasn't something real. And it could never be real as long as she didn't know about the nose, and as long as he was keeping this secret. She had loved him so perfectly and so honestly; he had never been loved this way before—for exactly who he was—and he treasured the way this felt so much that he craved more of it. He wanted to know it fully. But at the same time he understood that since he'd lied for so long, if he told her the truth about the nose now, she might not forgive him, and it might all go away. So he resolved to never tell her, no matter what. It would be his secret, his cross to bear.

But in the years that followed, every time she touched his chin, or kissed his face, or held his increasingly large body in her arms, his nose sizzled and burned—physically pricked and stung—and he wondered what it might be like if he told her everything. Maybe she would understand? Maybe it was not too late? Maybe they could have his old nose remade, just like it had once been, and then, with that, she would love him fully. One night he woke up screaming in his bed. In his sleep he'd had a hideous nightmare that the plastic surgeons put him under anesthesia without his consent, and they slipped all those awful parts back loosely under his skin, the big plastic chin, and the big plastic jaw. And they sewed his eyelids wide open with yarn, and squirted Jell-O into his cheeks, and in the place where his nose should have been, they jammed a big metal hook. In the dream he looked in the mirror and saw his face, and the only thing he was terrified about, the thing that woke him up shrieking in fear, was the thought that she might see his hook nose and know the real truth. And when he cried out for her to please not leave him in his sleep, she was there to hold him, and cradle him, and rock him back to sleep as she had on other nights when he'd had disturbing dreams. But on this night, he was so unsettled that he ran out of bed and turned on all the lights and studied his reflection in the mirror. Only it was too dark in their bedroom for him to believe he was seeing his true face, so he went into the bathroom, where the lights were brighter, and studied his reflection there, and then into the kitchen, where the lights were brighter yet, and looked there. And he finally was reassured that his face was okay, and he closed his eyes and touched his skin and breathed again.

But she had followed him into the kitchen, and she called out, "What are you doing?" she said. "Is something wrong?"

And then, "I have to tell you something," he said, just like that. "This is not my nose," he said. The words tumbled out of his mouth as quickly as that without his thinking about it, and when he said it he rubbed at the tip of his nose. "My nose had a long and ugly hook on it just like my mother's. This is a fake nose," he kept going. "It took the doctors three surgeries to make it. I should have told you long ago, but I didn't," he said. "I'm so sorry."

She looked down, and then out into the distance. "How could you have not told me that?" she said. "I would have loved you through anything. How could you have possibly not gotten that?"

"And now?" He saw something fall and slip away from her face. "And now?" he called out again. "What about now?" he screamed.

"I don't know," she said, turning away from him. From the moment she'd met him, she'd felt she was in a sort of wonderful trance, and now she felt that trance was suddenly broken. He didn't look the same to her anymore. She knew then that if he lied to her about the nose on his face, he could lie to her about anything, and that he would lie to her about anything, and she knew she would never be able to believe a single word he said to her again.

He had a very bad feeling then, as she started to walk away, that something had changed, and he couldn't imagine his life, not a single day of it, without her. He couldn't bear to think of it. He had to do something right away to show her that he was going to fix this mistake he made and repair the damage he'd done in lying to her. He had to prove to her that he was not just talk talking, that he was serious, that he was going to take action. Not someday, not tomorrow, but right now, this minute, he would fix it, or start fixing it, so they could get back to their love. Their beautiful and perfect and true love.

He grabbed scissors from the kitchen drawer, the ones they used to cut meat away from the bones, and he held them up, and he called out her name. He planned to take just a tiny bit off the tip as a gesture. He was no lunatic; he had no intention to cut the nose off his face. No—just a very small gesture to let her know he was serious, and going to set right what he had done wrong. He did it. There. He'd snipped off one tiny piece from the very tip of his nose. There was a burst of extraordinary pain that he had somehow not anticipated. But good, it was quickly washed away by a flood of adrenaline and then there was no pain at all.

"You said you'd love me through anything," he said. "Love me through this." The blood splattered everywhere. All over his mouth, metallic, and in between his teeth and onto the white counters with the soft gray veins, and all over the white tile floor. "You see. I made a mistake, but I'm fixing it for you," he said. "I'm fixing it right now.

I'll have the surgeon make my old nose back tonight. I will make this right. I will."

The look of horror on her face as if there were a complete stranger in her home. She ran and called 911. Came back. Held him in her arms and pressed a dish towel to his nose. "You've lost your mind," she was saying. "You're insane. You're insane."

"Please," he said. "Just give me one more chance." He was trying to catch her eye but could not. She would not look at him. They collapsed together onto the floor beside the kitchen table.

She held him very tight in her arms for what felt like a long while, and then let her grasp loosen. She said, "You'll never let anyone love you. You'll always keep one thing so you can say that they don't."

"That's not true," he said. "This is it, this is all of me, this is everything now." But even in his mad state he knew this wasn't entirely the case. There were still a few very tiny other small things she probably wouldn't care much about, but he hadn't mentioned them yet, and he wasn't entirely sure she would want to know about them anyway. He could see in her face that she understood all this now. She knew. And as the paramedics carried him away, he felt very sad and he knew she would not be there when he came back home.

He could have told her about the nose in the beginning, but he really didn't think she would have been able to look at it every day, really didn't think there was ever a version of the story where she would have had the nose remade and sewn on and loved him with it. It was hideous. Unordinarily so. One of his first memories as a young boy was recoiling at his dear mother's face while she was offering him her nipple, singing that Irish lullaby she was always singing. He prayed his nose would not be that way. But when he grew older so it was. So he became many of the things he hoped he was never going to be. Couldn't outrun it. And now she was gone and he would have to be some version of all the things he hated about himself—what?—alone?

He thought about what she'd said about how he'd always keep that one thing for himself. It rang true. Only, why would he do that? He had wanted to love her. He had wanted her to love him. He had wanted nothing more than those things. Why would he keep one thing for himself so he could tell himself *that* was the reason she didn't fully love him? If love was a promise two people made to each other to always show their true selves, then why was he always doing it with his fingers crossed behind his back? Where did that get him in the end? He didn't know. He wished he'd told her about the nose in the first place, done things differently. Why was it always so easy to see the right thing in retrospect?

He knew what he would do now. He would have the surgeon build back his old nose. Maybe he'd see her again one day on the street. She might not ever love him again. He didn't know if he could be that lucky twice. Maybe he could? He supposed it was possible. Anything was. But either way, there was a good chance he might see her again, and she'd see him with the nose, his real nose. And he'd know then what it felt like to be seen by her. And she might look at him from the front, and he'd tip his head so she could see him from another angle. And if she came close, he might feel that flash of electricity between them, and maybe she'd smile her mischievous smile, and touch his arm, and maybe she'd say, "I like it."

THE WIDOW

Shirley was already under the covers beginning her work, and Helen's tongue was on her neck, in her ear. Grace kept her mouth closed. In her sixty-eight years she'd never kissed a woman, and though there was something nice about it, something gentle, she wasn't going to start now. Helen was whispering things in her ear. So she was a *dirty talker*. Grace had heard about women like this, but in their forty-year friendship she never would have pegged Helen as one of them.

"Does that turn you on, baby?" Helen was saying. *Was she supposed to answer? Did people respond?* She moaned.

Under the covers Shirley was licking the inside of her thigh. Prior to that she'd licked the bottom of her stomach as lovingly as a puppy dog. This was the difference between men and women. When Henry, God rest his soul, would go under the covers, it was all business. The way he did it, she hated to admit it now, it always irritated her more than anything. But how she missed him. The months since he'd been gone had been wicked. She'd known grief before—her mother, her sister—but this was a surprise. This felt like terror. Often when she thought of him her heart would pound and she'd become breathless. She couldn't eat. She'd lost weight. Had stopped coloring her hair. It was almost all white now. Oh, what she wouldn't give for all those old things she'd spent her life complaining about. Lying awake in bed listening to him grind his teeth. Finishing dinner alone because he'd scarf down every meal too quickly. The musty smell of his T-shirts in the hamper. Having him play too rough with the kids—then later, the grandkids—before bedtime. Him there. There.

"Is there anything you like about me?" he'd asked her once, not too long ago. He had fixed the lock on the bathroom door and it broke the next day.

"No," she'd said, meaning it.

Now though, she understood—that had been all wrong.

Shirley had found just the right spot, and in her ear Helen said, "That's a girl, come on. Come for us," she said. "We want you to come." Grace let her mind go to Henry when he was still young, on top of her, the way he'd lose control like a wild animal at the end, how his face would turn red and the muscles in his arms would contract. How wild and strong and powerful he'd seem to her in those moments. She let herself slip away, fade away, so that she wasn't a person anymore, just a feeling. She was longing. She was fullness. She was stillness, satisfaction. She was more. She wanted more. *Please*. More.

WHERE WE USED TO LIVE

After my husband died, I moved back east to Syracuse, where I still had family, and I took a job at the answering service where I'd worked as a teen. I had advanced degrees; I could have gotten a nicer job. But I had a lot of money from the insurance, and I didn't want a job doing anything where I'd have to think. I wanted a time card. I wanted to log my hours, punch in and punch out, and be done with it. It was a good way to live. My daughter was six and going to the same school where I went, and it smelled exactly the same, a wonderful mix of crayon wax and Swedish meatballs. I needed something to do while she was gone all day. She'd been sad packing up our house in Los Angeles, but she was excited for all the snow I'd promised her we'd get in just a few months. It was her dream, she said, to make a snowman. So there was that. We got a little house with a huge backyard and lots of weeping willow trees.

The day-shifters at the answering service called themselves the Fatties. Beverly was the oldest and the clear leader. Everyone laughed at her idiotic jokes and let her decide where we ordered lunch. She was the day shift supervisor—the only difference in her responsibilities from what I could discern was that she told everyone when it was time to take their cigarette break. She took it very seriously, made herself a pathetic little chart that she'd study all morning.

We all sat at one large conference table, our computers in front of us, the middle a disgusting web of wires and plugs. Beverly sat at the head of the table, of course, and I sat just to her left, across from Gary, a father of four and a ninth-grade dropout, and Becky, a slut, who liked to tell us about her drunken exploits. Alice sat next to me, though she worked only a few days a week. She was the youngest of the Fatties, just nineteen, and getting close to finishing her first year of college at Syracuse University. She was fat, but only bottom fat. She had this big, enormous ass. Her face was pretty—black hair, pale skin, freckles, and icy blue eyes. She was pledging a sorority and always going to these big fraternity parties. The other day-shifters liked to tease her about this. They called her *sorority girl*, and when she'd come in they'd say stupid things like, "Delta Delta Delta. Can I help ya, help ya, help ya?" But they were dummies, all of them, and she wasn't, and so she didn't mind when they teased her.

Before he fell off the roof, my husband and I hadn't been getting along. I knew what our one and only problem was: I couldn't stand being around him. He annoyed me tremendously and constantly at every turn. I mean the guy drove me crazy. There was the way he'd quietly, almost inaudibly hum while he ate. You could almost not hear this little hum, but you *could* hear it. And at night, he made this clicking sound while he slept like if you put your tongue on the roof of your mouth and pulled down. I recorded it, played it for a friend of mine who was an ENT. She was perplexed, had never heard a person make this sound in their sleep before, thought maybe it had to do with his soft palate. He'd get these phrases in his head—song lyrics, or something he'd heard on TV—and he'd shout them out, over and over, all through any day. He had this habit of spoiling things for me. The news! Just before Lester Holt would begin, he'd pause the TV and tell me about every big story that happened that day. "Did you hear about the explosion in New Orleans?" he'd say. "No," I'd say. "Put it on, let me see," I'd say, gesturing toward the TV and raising my eyebrows rudely. But he'd tell me the whole thing anyway. I was careful to never touch him. I knew he'd take even the slightest touch from me as a come-on, and then he'd pester me to have sex until I gave in, mount me, hump me, apologize for being so quick, and fall asleep. I'd lay there naked, listening to the sounds of his clicks—*click, click, click*—and finish myself off, thinking of my high school boy-friend, whom I stalked, with alarming regularity, on Facebook. He was holding up well, Frank Vezza. Hair, and a not-too-fat middle.

I was holding up well too. I wasn't old. Young for a widow. I looked good. I heard someone say once that women are their most beautiful in their late thirties and I think this had to be true. It was the case for me. I had strong cheekbones, hazel eyes. People sometimes said I looked like a very famous actress. Strangers even said it. I could have found another husband if I wanted. I was no lost cause. Not some pity case. No one felt sorry for me.

My daughter was settling in. She liked her new school. She made some new friends and mentioned her father hardly ever at all. I knew this might not be a good thing, but she'd always been fiercely inde-pendent, my daughter, and so I let it be. I thought that becoming a mother was going to be more of a transformative experience. I thought it would be as earth-shattering as it seemed to be for some other women. Don't get me wrong—I loved the kid; she was won-derful; I wasn't one of those women who wanted to throw her child against the wall when she was an infant—I never had any of those kinds of impulses. I did everything I was supposed to, breastfed her for a year, took her to mommy-and-me classes, wore her in a baby carrier, all of it—you name it. But I always saw her as another person. She was simply another person who I loved very much. A person I had to take care of, and whom I would take care of—very well—for as long as she'd let me. She wasn't an answer to anything inside of me, is what I'm saying.

Alice liked to bring me little treats at work, usually chocolates. Nice brands too, not the garbage you find in drugstores. She didn't have a car, so I always gave her rides back to her dorm. On the way there she'd tell me all about her life, and all of her problems. She was a sweet girl, had the impression life was reasonable. Listening to her talk, I could almost remember what it was like to feel that way. She had been pledging her sorority for six weeks and had two to go. For the most part, the sisters were nice to her. Except for the one night, when her mom in the house, that's what she called her, her *mom*, came to her dorm in the middle of the night and brought her to the sorority house. When she got there, all the sisters were sitting in a big circle, in a dark room, holding lit candles. Alice and the other pledges sat on the floor in the middle of the circle, and the sisters asked them a bunch of questions about themselves—like what was their hometown, and what was their major? Who was their boyfriend, and what was their favorite drink? Any girl who didn't know the answers had to sit there all night with a bucket on her head. Luckily for Alice, she knew her stuff, and she got to go back to her dorm.

She had this boy she absolutely worshiped named Tyler who was clearly not that into her. She kept waiting for him to come around. She didn't know it yet, but at some point, probably after devoting two or three years of her life to elaborate fantasies of him, she'd figure out that she meant absolutely nothing at all—not a single thing—to him. Tyler was a few years older, in a fraternity, had a perfect chiseled jaw and the kind of sad eyes all women want to fix. I knew what he looked like because every time I looked over at her computer screen she was staring at a picture of him that she'd found online. She'd hit escape on her keyboard, and all of her calls would bounce over to me.

I didn't mind. I was efficient. I got the information I needed— name, number, and reason for call—and I dispatched it immediately and appropriately. I was good. I got to know some of the doctors whom we answered for, or, at least, know about them. Dr. Berman, for instance, was having an affair. He was an older guy, a real blob of a man with reddish hair and big puffy lips, and from his picture, I'd guess he was around sixty. His girlfriend would call the answering service directly, and we'd put her on hold, call his house, tell the wife there was an emergency, and then when Dr. Berman would get on the line, we'd patch the girlfriend through. Sometimes I'd hit mute and stay on. The girlfriend was young, a real firecracker. She was always mad at the doctor for something or else looking to hear about what he was going to do to her. She liked it rough. The doctor would tell her how he was going to tie her up and leave her naked somewhere, that kind of thing.

I had an affair once. It was brief and revolting. The guy had rotting teeth and breath that smelled like cauliflower. He was just filthy— greasy hair and pockmarks all over his face. Thick gunk under his fingernails. I met him at a gardening center around the corner from where we used to live; he worked there. He asked me if he could help get some plants into my car, and I could tell that he wanted me, and it made me sick, and then it made me sad that he thought he was in my league, then somehow I found myself wanting to lick every inch of him. And so I did. Just a few times, and that was it. No one ever knew. I didn't make any big drama about it.

I never wanted to lick every inch of my husband.

My daughter was the only one with him when the accident happened. She ran in, panting. "Come quick," she said, like in a movie. "Daddy is bleeding," she said. "He fell off the roof."

Thirty seconds later I was outside in our yard. My husband was sitting there, holding his head, and blood was slipping between his fingers. There was an actual puddle of blood on the ground where he must have been lying. But somehow, I didn't immediately understand the gravity of the situation. "Are you okay?" I said. My heart pounded, but I also felt totally fine. I had the sense this would be like all the other times in my life when I thought something was a terrible emergency, and it turned out to be not so bad.

"Get me a towel," he said. "I just need a towel."

I ran to get it, told my daughter to stay inside, but I had this funny feeling we were all being dramatic, that I was running for show, that I was acting like a woman in crisis, but I was not actually a woman in crisis, and it was going to turn out fine. It was not the first time in my life I had this feeling. I didn't know who I was performing for. Myself? My daughter? The universe? When I got back outside my husband was standing up, walking toward the house, still with his hand on his head, the dark blood oozing through his fingers. Seeing him standing, I felt smug. *I knew it,* I thought. *He's okay.* I gave him the towel, let him lean on me as we moved toward the house. He was moving very slowly and he started to talk.

"I put it over there," he said. "We can go get it, it's just over there." He pointed up toward the top of a tree. There was a cheerful bounce in his voice, like he was telling a joke or reading a nursery rhyme. "That's not all," he said. "That's not it." Then he laughed, "Yes, yes," he said. "But only when I was a kid."

"What are you saying?" I said. "What are you talking about?" Inside my chest my heart started to do unusual things. I felt the blood rush away from my feet.

"The little blue," he said. He laughed and went on, "on the blocky-doo," as if he were reading a poem. Then he said quickly, "I'm just going to lie down right here," and he lay down, and his eyes rolled toward the back of his head for a few moments, then closed, and I saw that the towel was completely soaked through, and that was when I screamed for my daughter to get my phone, get me my phone, to go get me my phone, and I called 911.

He was unconscious when they carried him off. By the time they got him to the hospital, he was dead.

One Friday, a few of the night-shifters got the flu, and Alice and I agreed to do the three-to-eleven. My sister was watching my daughter at my house; she'd planned to stay the night. After work, I dropped Alice off at one of her fraternity parties.

When we got there: "Okay," she said. "I know you're going to say no," she said. "But hear me out," and then, "It would mean so much to me—"

"Oh, no," I said. "What does she want from me now?"

"Come in with me," she said. "I would *love* the sisters to meet you." She looked at me and held up her hands as if she were praying. "I've told them so much about you," she said. "Please, please, please, please, please, please. You'd only have to stay for a few minutes."

I was decades older than Alice—she seemed like a literal baby, but I could tell that she looked up to me, that I was the kind of person she wanted to be. She didn't have much family, and I knew she saw me as a slightly older and cooler version of herself. "Okay, I'll do it," I said, taking off my bulky coat. "But I'm not doing any keg stands," I said. I rubbed some of the stray eyeliner from underneath my eyes and opened the car door. "And I'm not blowing any frat boys," I said.

She caught my eye. "Is this your night off?" she said. Then, as we got out of the car, "Careful over here," she said. "Lots of black ice."

Inside, the music thudded, and the room was dark and filthy. A few old velour couches were pushed against the walls to make room for a dance floor. A pack of half-naked girls rushed right over to Alice and dragged her out onto it. "These are my sisters," she called back to me as they pulled her away. She put her arms around them and they began to dance. Britney Spears's "Baby One More Time" was playing. I knew every single word of the stupid song, but they were listening ironically. To them it was a classic, or a joke, or both. I'd been to parties like this, in college and after, and I could almost remember having as much fun as they all seemed to be having. But only almost.

A few minutes later a dark-haired boy in a Yankees cap came over to me. "Hey," he said. "I haven't seen you before," he said, squinting. He had light eyes, a little beard, and full lips. "Are you a DG?"

"No," I said, and just then the song "Baby Got Back" came on. Alice moved to the center of the dance floor and started going at it like she owned the place. I was surprised—at work she was kind of quiet. I never saw her as the type to dance the way she was dancing, never thought those giant hips of hers would move the way they were moving. Another girl came behind her and started grinding her. After a moment of watching I started to tell the boy about the answering service, but then I got a whiff of his cologne. It was a musty odor, just barely covered with Axe body spray. I couldn't believe guys still used that stuff. I thought about how wild young men were in bed, like animals at the end, their faces red and covered in sweat. "I'm a Tridelt," I said.

"Cool," he said, looking at me, and then just past me.

I said, "Are you—"

He shook his red plastic cup. "Hey," he said. "I gotta grab another beer," he said. "It was good to meet you," and he tapped my shoulder.

My cheeks stung. Alice came over. "There's this thing I need to do," she said. "You know how next week is initiation? Well, there's this one thing I need to do first." She looked upset, as though she might start to cry. "They just told me. Listen, I'm just going to run upstairs for a few minutes," she said. "But I'll be right back down."

"Wait. Where are you going?" I said. "Is everything okay?"

"It's nothing," she said. "It's just this guy. They want me to—He has to tell them I—" she said. She was quiet for a moment. "He has to give me a recommendation."

"Come on, Alice," I said. "Don't do things you don't want to do." I suddenly felt like her mother or her big sister. I had an impulse to drag her out of there, but I wasn't her mother or her sister, and it wasn't my place.

"Don't look at me like that," she said. "If I just do this one thing," she said, "I'll be a sister, and then—" She looked off. "I'm just gonna be right back," she said. She started to walk away and turned. "It's really not that big of a deal. It's not like I have to—I'm just gonna use my hand."

"Okay," I said. "I'll be here." I stood near a window and looked out, then felt like I needed some fresh air, so I went out onto the porch. It had started to snow, and everything smelled icy and blue. The tiny hairs inside my nose froze. I took a deep breath, looked around. I'd missed winter. The snowflakes were big and fluffy. It was the kind of snow that crunched under your feet, I could tell. The next day, I thought, I'd call out of work, and let my daughter stay home from school, and we'd go in the backyard and make a snowman. Hell, we'd make a whole snow family. I made a mental note to stop at the store and buy a bag of carrots on the way home. The Price Chopper on Erie Boulevard would probably still be open. If there was enough snow, I might wake my daughter up tonight, why not—I could wake her up tonight, and keep her home tomorrow too, both things; she'd love it.

Alice was back very quickly, maybe she was gone just ten minutes, I wasn't sure. She seemed okay, though she didn't look at me. I told her I could drive her to her dorm, and she agreed.

As we walked down the porch stairs, "Alice," a voice called from a little ways down the street.

"Holy shit," she said. "That's Tyler." She clutched my arm. "I can't see him now," she said. "Not like this. Not now." She fussed with her hair, pulled a lipstick from her pocket and rubbed it over her lips.

"You look fine," I said. "You're perfect," I said. "Come on." I held on to her so we wouldn't slip on the ice.

When he got closer, he asked, with a goofy smile, "Heading home already?"

"Long day," she said. "You?"

"I'm parked right there," he said, gesturing toward a gray hatchback. "I'm heading up," he said. "You want a lift?" He was different in person. Handsome, yes. But not in the way I'd expected. What I'd decided about him from looking at that photo—well, there was tenderness in his eyes, I could see that.

I said hello to him, told them I had to get going, and went to my car across the street.

After I closed the door, I adjusted my mirror so I could see them. They stood there awhile, face-to-face. Her arms around his neck, and his around her waist; they were talking. He was very tall in person. She was looking up at him in a way I'd never looked at anyone. And he was looking at her the same way.

Once, a very long time ago, before we moved away from here, and before we had our daughter, my husband woke in the middle of the night. It was the first snowfall of the season, a night like this. He put on his coat and boots and ran outside, like a lunatic, and made me a row of snow angels in the backyard just in front of our bedroom window. When he came back in, he stripped off all his clothes, and I took mine off too, and we melted into each other. And how good it felt, that night, his body so cold, mine so warm. We had some things.

Looking at Alice now, I could almost feel the excitement she must have been feeling being in Tyler's arms. Anything could still happen between them. Anything at all. What a wonderful feeling it was:

possibility. What could be better. They started to kiss. Softly, playfully, at first—he bit her lip, and she laughed—then they kissed deeply. The snow was falling. Coming down hard. Their hair was turning white. Looking at them, a strange thing happened to me: I could feel time. It seemed as though if I wanted to, I could reach out and touch it. I could feel the years of my life passing. So much of my life seemed to be looking forward to something that never came, but now, somehow, it all seemed to be behind me.

I sat there and watched for a while longer as they kissed. I turned the key in the ignition, but for some reason, I could not pull away. I closed my eyes, then, and willed Alice to stay there, just like that, in Tyler's arms, in the snow, for as long as she could—all night, forever.

HELP WILL BE HERE SOON

It was what you heard. I was the woman in the living room that the car crashed into. I was sending an email, who I was emailing is not important, it is not relevant. I was on the couch, Johnny was in the kitchen getting his second gin, his third, who cared. The car came through the wall and stopped just before it hit me. The sound is what I remember most, spectacular, like it was coming from within, like I was being cracked open from within. I thought it was an earthquake, the one we'd all been waiting for. It took me a while to understand, no, the earth was okay, it was just here, just our house. Johnny came running over and went to the car. I sat there on the couch, not moving. Johnny pulled the driver out first and the driver looked okay, solid, though he was asleep. I took a sip of my Diet Coke. The ice clanked the sides of the glass. Johnny went around then and tried to get the passenger out. Now Johnny was struggling. I thought the leg must be stuck, that the car must have pinched down. I considered that the man might have been very heavy, though he did not look partic- ularly heavy. Johnny worked away, quietly pulling. The car radio was going. When Johnny and I were a lot younger we used to go fishing, and the way he was pulling at the passenger made me think of the times when his line would get stuck. The room was filled with smoke, but there were no flames. One wall was down, part of another. Deep outside I saw the moon, stars. Johnny pulled and pulled, and after a while, the passenger came loose. He dragged the passenger over right next to where he'd put the driver. The driver awoke then, and he was screaming. He was screaming so loud but I couldn't understand what he was saying; you see, he didn't speak English. So the driver was screaming and screaming right into the passenger's face, then he grabbed the passenger and shook him hard, and when the passenger stayed still, he went over him, started pressing on his chest, breathing into his mouth. It was only then, seeing them there, like that, mouth to mouth, that I understood they were lovers, married. Johnny was on the phone now, calling 911. There was a lot of chaos; look, all this was happening fast. I let my eyes stay on the passenger. For his part he was the most calming presence in the room, the only one not caus- ing a scene. I kept my eyes on him, let Johnny, the screaming driver, the smoke, the distant sirens—all of it—melt away. The passenger was wearing a sports jacket, jeans. He had dark hair, a prominent jaw; he was handsome. I sat there watching to see if he would move, or gasp, or bleed, or anything, but he did not. Then like that I understood that he was dead. A man had come into our living room, and minutes later, he was dead. The driver must have realized this too, for he crumbled into a ball and started to wail. Johnny didn't hesitate; he went over and sat down next to him on the floor. The driver curled into Johnny's chest, and Johnny put his arms around him. "Don't worry," he told the man, caressing his head as gently as he'd caressed our daughter's head when she was an infant. "Help will be here soon," he was saying.

I watched them rocking, Johnny and the driver, saw the dead man lying still, and here's the thing, I felt grateful in that moment, is what

I'm saying. I felt grateful that Johnny was my husband, this man, and no one else. I felt grateful that we were home, in our own living room, even as the walls came down, and the frigid night air all around us made our skin burn.

Our Lives Without Each Other

On the first morning of our stay, a good-looking couple, dressed mostly in black, sat down beside us, at the other wooden table facing the window. After a few moments Beth stopped eating her omelet and looked out the window, lips pursed. I had no intention of giving in to her, but then she started with her sighing.

"Yes," I said finally, holding a forkful of French toast in front of my mouth. It was our ten-year wedding anniversary. Beth had convinced me to drive forty minutes outside of town to the bed and-breakfast in Skaneatcles where I got down on one knee and proposed eleven years earlier. My mother drove in to watch our daughter, Rose, and now we had two days to "reconnect," as Beth had put it.

She looked around, then mouthed the words, "They're. Not. Married," opening her mouth wider, I thought, than was necessary. Beth was a big-boned woman with pale skin and wavy reddish hair. She'd been home with our daughter for the past two years and there was nothing that pleased her more than some gossip.

"And," I said.

"Not. To. Each. Other." The snow falling outside was heavy on the pine trees and the barn. I didn't care who the people next to us were married to. It had been a rough few years. Before the baby, Beth slipped into a depression that left her in bed and unable to speak for months. The baby brightened things, but it had not been the same between Beth and me. You'd think having a kid would bring you closer, but what it does is the opposite. When I was home from work, Beth needed a break, or she had something she needed to do. It seemed there was never a time the three of us were in the same room together. I shrugged and took a sip of my coffee. Beth squinted as though I'd done her some personal offense. She went back to listening to the couple, I could tell.

I went back to my French toast. Now I was listening too.

"Tell me, tell me, tell me," the young woman was saying. Her black hair hung midway down her back, and when she talked her mouth went to the left.

"No, girl," the man said. "Not here."

"You're killing me," she said. "You know that, don't you?"

"Later," he said, moving closer. Now they were saying things in hushed voices that I couldn't make out. The morning sunlight on the snow was blinding through the big French windows. They were holding all four hands on the table. A diamond on her ring finger sparkled and shot rainbows through the room.

"It's so nice to be able to do this," she said, looking at their hands on the table. He leaned over and kissed her. "That too," she said, laughing. Then he leaned in for a longer kiss.

I looked back to Beth, whose eyes were wide open. She had not been able to lose the last of the baby weight, and her cheeks were fuller than they used to be. "How do you know, anyway?" I asked.

"I heard him say, *my wife.*"

The owner of the bed-and-breakfast, who was also our waitress, came over and asked if everything was okay, if we wanted anything else. "Everything is wonderful," Beth said, looking around. "Just wonderful."

"Isn't it though?" the young woman said, leaning to see. "Wonderful though. Isn't it?"

"Yes," Beth said, turning. Through the window a tire filled with snow swung in an oak tree. "Pretty as a picture," she added, shifting toward the couple. "You all aren't from around here, are you?" she asked. It always surprised me how outgoing Beth could be given the proper motivation.

The man turned to be part of the conversation now too. He was handsome, with dark shoulder-length hair and a full beard. He could have been a lead singer. He wore a black T-shirt and a wool cap on his head.

"No," the young woman said, and they looked at each other and smiled. "We're visiting from New York," she went on. "Ed had a conference at the university." Ed put down his coffee and extended a stiff hand. I stood for a moment to shake it, and Beth waved. From the other side of the table, the young woman lifted her hand and waved. "I'm Katie," she said.

"Nice to meet you, Katie," Beth said. "Hi, Ed." Her face filled with color when she looked at him. "We live just outside of Syracuse," she said. Then a few moments passed with no one saying anything.

I said, "It's our wedding anniversary this weekend."

"Oh, well, congratulations," Katie said.

"How long is that now?" Ed asked.

"Ten years," Beth told them

"Imagine *that*," Katie said, widening her eyes, and we laughed. Then she made her fingers into a gun and shot herself in the temple, and we all laughed again.

That afternoon, Beth and I milled around the town. We went into the small shops the way we used to when we were first dating, and looked at the displays. Beth bought a green wooden sign that had carved into it ALWAYS KISS ME GOODNIGHT and in the art store she bought a painting of the town on a winter afternoon that looked exactly like it did today. We walked by the lake, which was mostly frozen. Large blocks of ice gathered at the edge and clanked together each time the water beneath them stirred. We stood and watched the ice move for a while. An older man walked by whistling something familiar: Elvis's "Fools Rush In." My heart quickened, but Beth's face seemed okay. This was something we avoided now: music. Since the great depression the smallest thing could set her off. I could see her dangling sometimes, hanging in that delicate space, on the brink of slipping back under.

"I feel like we never left," she said after a while. I knew what she meant. I had the same feeling standing there beside her in front of the lake just the way we had so long ago. That eleven years of life had passed between then and now seemed like a joke. Maybe we'd been gone a month. I could believe that. A month. No more.

For lunch we went to a restaurant with high ceilings and a large stone fireplace. The smell of the burning wood made me feel cold. Beth ordered a Thanksgiving sandwich, which was turkey, stuffing, and cranberry, with sweet potato french fries on the side. I ordered grilled chicken. Before our sandwiches came, Beth excused herself to call my mother. This was the first time we'd left Rose for an over-night. When she came back she said everything was going well, then she went to her sandwich without looking up. Sometimes when Beth and I go out to eat, I intentionally don't say anything to see if she will. We have made it through entire meals not saying a word. When I mention it after, she tells me she was relaxed, or enjoying herself.

Beth was quiet. I asked her, finally, "How do you like being a mother?" It was the only thing I could think to say. She looked at the fire, then back at me. "Most of the time," she said, "I love it. There's nothing I'd rather be doing." She took a bite of her sandwich and stared at her plate. "What is it they say?" she said. "The days are long, but the years are short?"

I nodded. In our first few months with Rose I couldn't count how many strangers had shared this sentiment with us.

"It's true," she said. "Sometimes I'm counting the hours till you get home, because I'm so exhausted I can barely keep it together," she said. "But now she's two." She had another bite of her sandwich. Her gaze went through the restaurant, over the empty tables, and out into the cold. "I should have taken more pictures," she said. The fire crackled. The waitress walked to our table, filled our water glasses, and left again. Beth took a drink. "What about you?" she said at last. "How do you like being a father? She loves you. You should see how happy she is when she hears you coming in."

"I love her too," I told her. "She's an amazing kid," I said. Beth looked at me, and I added, "Thanks to you."

It was true. Beth had made all the decisions. She'd read the books and decided the kind of parents we would be. It was Beth who decided the baby would sleep in our bed with us. "People think it will make them more dependent, but it actually makes them more independent," she'd told me. I went along with it. I had no intuition for what was best. Beth was always telling me how to be and what to say to the baby. When she'd fall, for instance, all I had to do, Beth told me, was tell her what happened. "Narrate," she'd say. "Just knowing what happened, and knowing you saw what happened, will be enough to calm her down."

I loved Rose. Loved her more than I thought possible. But the truth was, I didn't feel like a dad. The waitress gave us the check and I said, "I love being a father."

———————

In our room we lay on the bed. Beth had a magazine that she'd brought from home, and I had the new Stephen King book I'd been trying to get through all year. There were two bedrooms at the Stone House and we were in the same one we had last time, just as I'd requested. The room was pretty. All the comforts of home, and unchanged since we'd been there last. The walls were painted a soft blue. There was a dark antique dresser on one wall with gold handles on the drawers. Over the dresser hung an antique mirror, and at the foot of the bed was a hook rug with a muted floral pattern. Just past that, in front of the window, was a wingback chair and a small antique table with spindle legs. On the table was a vase filled with dried lavender. Beth kept the window open a few inches because the smell of the antiques made her throat tickle. An icy breeze hung near it. Every now and then, Beth's foot would bump mine, and when she got up for a drink, she gave my shoulder a squeeze.

When she came back to the bed I said, "We should have sex."

"I don't know," Beth said, scrunching her face.

This was more encouragement than usual. "Come on," I said. "It's been months. We're here to reconnect," I said. I got behind her and ran my fingers through her hair. I kissed her neck and her shoulder. When she didn't protest, I let my hand go over her breast. "Let's be spontaneous," I said. "Come on."

After a minute she turned to me and closed her eyes. She moved her hand along my side. "Okay," she said. "If you really want to." She stood and walked into the bathroom. I pulled my jeans off and tossed them onto the floor.

I could hear Beth fumbling through her toiletries. A minute later, she came back without any clothes on. "Don't look," she said, as she made her way to the bed. She crossed her arms over her breasts.

"You're beautiful," I said, taking off my shirt. Beth had always been beautiful. She'd become self-conscious since the baby, but she still turned me on. After some time messing around we began. From the look on her face, it was hard to tell if she was enjoying it or not, so I kept my eyes closed. When we were dating, years back, Beth was the best sex I'd ever had. She had a wild streak in her that always surprised me. We did it in a park, once, in broad daylight. Another time, she gave me head in a department store changing room. But I had not seen that side of Beth in years. Our sex now was not young people's sex. It was mature sex. Efficient and punctual. Responsible and purposeful. Satisfactory. But I wasn't going to complain. It was still better than no sex. When we were done, I rolled onto my back. Beth snuggled beside me. "Thank you," I said, patting her shoulder.

In a soft voice she said, "I told you not to thank me."

"I'm sorry," I said.

"Don't apologize," she said.

And it was quiet.

I drifted off. I dreamed I was helping my mother unpack her groceries in our old kitchen. This was not unusual: I was always dreaming of something from long ago. My age in life had exceeded the age I saw myself as in my dreams.

Beth had her shirt back on and she was standing with her head to the wall. "I can hear them," she said. Her eyes wild.

"Hear who?" I asked.

"Katie and Ed," she said. "From this morning. They're having a fight."

I found my boxers at the bottom of the bed, slipped them on, and went over to the wall next to her.

"I just don't understand," Katie was saying in a loud voice. "It doesn't add up."

"These things you're worried about," Ed said, "they're monsters under the bed. I love *you*," he said. "I'm here with *you*. I—"

"Why is she texting you?" Katie said.

"She wanted to thank me," Ed said. "That's all."

"Why does she even have your number?" Katie said. "It doesn't make sense," she said again.

"Things are different than when you were in college, girl," Ed said. "Students text their professors now."

It got quiet. After a few moments, Katie said, "I just don't know what we're doing anymore. I don't even know what you want."

"We'll figure it out," Ed said. "It'll become clear in time," he said. Then, after a few moments, he added, "Look at me, girl. No one is going to get hurt." He said, "I promise."

For a while there was nothing. Minutes later we heard Katie moaning. Quiet at first, and then loud.

Now my eyes were wild. "Sounds like someone made up," I whispered.

"Hey," Beth said, tilting her head and moving closer. "Come on," she said into my neck.

"What's gotten into you?" I said, as she got down on her knees.

Later that afternoon, there was a knock at the door.

"Yes?" I called out. "Can I help you?" I said.

"It's Katie," a voice said. "We met in the dining room this morning," she said.

Beth stood up and checked herself in the mirror. I opened the door. Katie had changed her clothes. Now she was wearing red lipstick and a low-cut black sweater. Her hair smelled of vanilla.

"How's it going?" I said.

"I hope I'm not bothering you," she said. "I forgot my iPhone charger. You don't happen to have one," she said, "do you?" She peeked in at Beth. "I asked downstairs but they don't have one."

"Of course," I said. I went to the small table, unplugged my charger, and handed it to her.

"Oh, great," she said. "You're saving my life," she told me.

"Don't mention it," I said.

"Glad to help," Beth called out.

"I'll bring it right back," she said, holding it in the air with a shake. She started to walk away, then stopped and turned. "Hey," she said. "Would you guys want to have a drink with us?"

I looked at Beth, and she shrugged. "Sure," I said.

"Cool," she said. "We're right here," she said. "Next door. In about an hour?" she said.

"Works for us," Beth said.

Katie and Ed had a different view. Their windows looked out onto the back of the house; ours faced the side. The darkness was different. Brighter. From their window I could see into the deep woods. I thought of the animals running wild in the freezing night.

"Wine okay?" Ed asked, holding a bottle of red in his hand.

"Perfect," I said. Their room was bigger too. On the other side of their bed was an area with a couch, a small coffee table, and two wingback chairs. Over their four-poster bed hung a lace canopy. Romantic. One of them had set candles all around the room, and the flickers made my mind go to fireflies on summer nights when I was a kid.

"Wine is good for me," Beth said.

Ed sat on the couch and poured the wine into the small glasses. He was wearing a plaid shirt now, buttoned all the way to his neck, and gray jeans. He held a glass out to Beth, and she walked over and sat beside him on the couch.

"You guys have a better view," I said, my eyes fixed on the window.

"We saw some deer last night. A mama and a baby," Katie said, getting up from the edge of the bed where she'd been sitting. She walked over to the window beside me. The smell of her vanilla hair made me drunk. "Right there," she said. "See where those piles of hay are? They were feeding right there."

"Wow," I said, looking out into the night.

After a minute Katie said, "So what do you do?"

"I'm an accountant," I said.

"A suit?" Ed said from over on the couch with a laugh in his voice.

"Yes," I said, feeling suddenly ashamed. "You?" I asked him.

"I write," he said, lifting his eyebrows.

"And he teaches," Katie added.

"A writer," Beth said, perking up. "Have you written anything we would have read?" she asked.

I shot her a look. In all the time I'd known Beth, she'd only read one book and it was *The Alchemist*.

"Unlikely," he said.

"All of his students are in love with him," Katie said with a laugh. Then to Beth she added, "I don't remember any of my professors looking like that."

Beth's face filled with color. Her eyes went to Ed and then back to Katie. "No," she said. She looked at Ed again, and then over to me. My stomach turned at the thought of how I must look in comparison. I had not been to the gym since before the baby, and what was left of my hair was starting to go gray now.

Ed looked up at Katie. "Girl," he said. "Let's not start with that."

She went to him and stood behind him. She worked his long hair with her hands as if she were going to put it in a ponytail. "Oh," she said. "I'm just saying you're very handsome." She leaned down and kissed his neck. When she bent, I saw the full shape of her breasts. Under the lace of her bra was nipple. A chill went through my spine. I looked away. "You don't have to get all mad," she said. She came around and sat down on the chair next to me.

"What about you?" I said to her. "What do you do?"

"Not much," Katie said. "Not much right now," she said, looking off. "I want to act."

"That's how we met," Ed said. "Katie was a grad student."

"Oh," Beth said. "So you were you her professor?"

"No," Ed said. "That's just how we met."

"Do you guys have kids?" Katie asked me.

"One," I said. "A daughter."

Beth stood and went to her purse. "Her name is Rose," she said, pulling out her phone.

"No, Beth—" I said.

"Don't be silly," Katie said. "We want to see." Beth showed the picture. "She looks like you," Katie said to me. "That smile."

"Look at those squinty eyes," Ed said. He took his own phone from the table and flashed a picture at Beth. "This is my baby," he said.

Beth laughed. "Oh," she said, "stop." Then she added, "What's her name?"

"Tilly," he said. "Of course," he said with a smile. He showed me the picture next: a Yorkie in a Hawaiian shirt.

Ed's phone rang. He looked at it, but he let it keep ringing. "I never hit decline," he said to both of us, as though we'd asked. "Everybody knows they've been declined if it goes to voicemail after two rings," he said. "It's like saying, 'Fuck you.'"

"You're so right," Beth said, laughing.

"Just wait it out," Ed went on. "Have some fucking manners."

Beth laughed harder.

"Very funny," I said, though I had the sense he'd said this same thing a thousand times.

We sat for a while and drank our wine. Katie did most of the talking. The nonsense small talk you make with people you know you'll never see again. It wasn't much different, I supposed, than the kind of talk we had with our closest friends. Beth jumped in every now and then with one of her stories. Whenever we were around other people, Beth had a habit of selling me out. It was her thing. No matter the subject, she'd find a way to bring it around to how stupid I was. Ed didn't say much, but he was paying close attention, laughing at all the right moments, egging her along.

". . . And forget it when he has to assemble something," Beth was saying, a laugh in her voice. "I wait for it," she said. "Every single time, I'll hear him say, 'Huh, that part must be missing,' or, 'Huh, I guess they included an extra screw.'"

Everyone laughed. It wasn't my fault every piece of junk we bought was defective. I was relieved she didn't start up with her favorite story: how I'd bought her ring with store credit after my first engagement fell through.

After about an hour, Ed went to pour himself another glass. He eyed Katie when there was nothing left.

"Oh," Katie said, "no," she said. "I want to keep on hanging out." She caught my eye with sadness. "We never do anything like this."

"Yeah," Beth said, looking at me. "We don't either. I'm having fun," she said.

I tried to think of the last time I heard her say that. All I could come up with was a wedding we went to five or six years back with her college friends. In your thirties, having fun gets swapped for having a nice dinner out. After you have a kid, even that goes.

"Well, who's coming with me to the store?" Ed said, standing.

Katie looked at him. "Ed," she said. "You can't drive."

"I'm fine," he said. "I had one glass."

"Two," she said. "Before they came? Remember?"

"I'm fine," Ed said. "Really." He grabbed a black coat from the closet, pulled it on, then grabbed his wool cap.

Katie looked at me, and then at Beth. She looked helpless and young then, and it occurred to me that she was probably still in her twenties.

"Why don't we all go," Beth said. "I could use some fresh air," she said. "Maybe we can grab something to eat while we're out."

"You may have a difficult time getting back up the driveway with the ice," the owner said to us as we were leaving. "If you do, put your car in neutral and give it full gas," she said.

"Thanks," Ed said.

The snow was coming down hard. It was heavy snow, and it crunched under our feet as we made our way to Ed's car. On the path leading to the cars, the high branches of the pine trees touched. Katie and Ed went through first. "I now pronounce you man and wife," I heard her whisper to him, as though it were their wedding aisle.

I squeezed into the back of Ed's car behind him, and Beth got in behind Katie. Ed went slow until we got on the main road, then he took off. In twenty minutes we were parked outside the 7-Eleven on Eric Boulevard. It was the only thing open. In high school, this was the very place we'd hang out on weekend nights and pay strangers to buy us beer.

Ed went into the store. We were quiet for a minute, then Katie spoke. "I want to tell you guys something," she said. "Ed and I— we're married to other people. What I mean is—Christ, I don't know if I've ever said this out loud, but—we're having an affair." She turned and looked at us, twirling her black hair around her finger.

"It's your business," I said. "You don't need to worry about that with us."

"We've tried to end it," she said. "We have. But we love each other too much. It's not as easy as that."

"How'd it get started?" Beth said. "That's the thing."

"Beth," I said, giving her a look.

"I know how this is going to sound," Katie said. "But we're soul mates," she said. "It's true."

"It could be true," I said. This part, I admit, I didn't believe. Why was it that everyone found their soul mate when they were married to someone else?

She started to smile and looked at me. "Ed's been talking about how someday we're gonna—" We heard a twinkling sound, and Ed's phone lit up. Katie stopped talking and grabbed it. She looked at us, at the 7-Eleven, then back at the phone. "I know his code," she said, as she punched it in. She read his text, then looked out the window. A moment passed. She put her head down and closed her eyes. "Fucking asshole," she whispered.

"What is it?" Beth asked, leaning forward.

"Oh," she said. "One of his girls," she said. "Ed has all these girls after him," she said. "They throw themselves at him. I've seen it."

"That must be hard," Beth said.

I felt a pang of envy, and wished, for a moment, that Beth could relate.

Something occurred to me, then. Katie wasn't jealous of his wife. It seemed she worried about every girl except the one he slept with every night. "He's with you though, right?" I said.

"I don't know," Katie said. "Sometimes I think he is. Other times, I just don't know," she said. She was quiet.

Through the window, under the neon lights of the 7-Eleven, we could see Ed waiting in a long line with a six-pack in each hand.

Katie went on. "It's been almost two years," she said. "Ed keeps telling me that our real life is going to start soon."

"Your real life?" Beth asked.

"That's what we call it," she said, "when we talk about our future. I guess that makes this—everything else—our fake life." She laughed and then looked down the boulevard. Lights sparkled and blurred. Cars flew by splashing slush behind them. "You guys aren't even here right now," she said, sort of laughing. "None of this is even happening."

"Don't take this the wrong way," Beth said, "but what about his wife? What about your husband? Where do they fit into all this?"

I shifted my weight away from her and looked out my window. Just past the pumps of gasoline a billboard read: YOU ONLY LIVE ONCE, MAKE SURE IT'S ENOUGH.

"His wife?" Katie said. "I don't know much about her," she said. She said, "We try not to talk about our lives without each other." She was quiet. In the store Ed was up next to check out. "I know it's hard to understand," she said, turning the diamond ring on her finger. "The best I can explain it is to say I feel like I'm at home when I'm with Ed. With my husband, it's like being at someone else's house," she said.

"I don't get that," Beth said. "I'm sorry but I just don't," she said.

I understood. I'd had the feeling before of being a visitor in my own life. Had found myself uncertain why I was the guy mowing the big lawn, surprised that the baby crying, "Dada Dada," was looking at me.

"He's a good man," Katie said. "My husband. I never worry with him," she said. "And I don't not love him," she said. "It's just a different love with Ed. I feel so much."

"I see," Beth said. "That makes sense."

I caught her eye for a moment, then she turned her head and looked through her window.

Ed opened the door and handed the bag to Katie.

Before he pulled away, she tossed his phone at him. "You should call Madison," she said, looking through her window, away from him.

"What?" Ed said. "What are you talking about?" He grabbed his phone and ran his thumb over the screen. "Come on, girl," he said. "You're hacking my phone, now?" He tipped his head toward us. "Can we not do this right now, please?"

She said, "It's okay. I told them." Then she added, "They don't know anyone." She went on looking through her window. "Go ahead," she said after a moment, "call your girlfriend."

"Fuck," he said. He jerked the car into reverse and skidded away from the store. "I'll never understand you, girl," he said. He got onto the boulevard, then, in a minute, onto the highway. Neither of them said anything, but his car was picking up surprising speed.

After a minute, Katie said, "Ed," pleading. "Slow down. Will you please slow down?" she said. But he kept his foot on the gas.

Beth took her hand from her pocket and reached for my hand. "Do you want me to drive, buddy?" I said.

His directional clicked on, and I felt a wave of relief, but as he switched lanes, the car slid and lost control. It kept swerving and swerving and missing things. It went pretty far considering the speed. But that's how it is when you're out of control, you keep going like that longer than you think you would. When it finally stopped we'd crossed the median. We were on the other side of the highway facing the wrong way. Beth started to scream. "Get over, get over," she said, "move." Snowflakes hit the windshield, and the wipers went all the way left and all the way right. Horns blasted by us, their high beams blinding. Ed jerked the car into gear and took off for the other side, but he overshot and smashed into a tree. Katie's head cracked into the dashboard. The whole thing took about a minute. Then, like that, it was done.

Beth was okay, I could see. Neither of us were hurt.

Ed was unhurt too. He reached for Katie and asked her if she was all right. When she didn't respond, he stayed calm. He put his hands around her neck and held it in place. "Girl," he said. "Wake up," he said. When she didn't move, he said, "Call 911," and Beth did.

A minute later Katie opened her eyes and started to scream. She would not stop screaming.

"Girl," Ed yelled over her. "We had an accident. The car hit a tree, and you hit your head on the dashboard. You're bleeding, but you're going to be okay."

"Ed," she said. "Ed." Her eyes were closing again.

He held her neck straight and stared into her face. Blood dripped from her forehead onto her legs. It was too much blood. More blood than it seemed could fit in her head.

"We're going to be okay," he said.

I saw her body relax. Maybe he was right. Maybe everything would be okay.

"Listen to me, girl," he said with uncommon tenderness. "I'm always going to take care of you," he said.

When he said this, Beth put her face in her hands and started to cry.

"Are you okay?" I said. "Beth, are you hurt?"

"I'm okay," she said, but from the tone of her voice I understood that she wasn't. Something had shifted, taken over. Maybe the accident was too much. "It's going to be okay, Beth," I said. "We're okay," I said. I put my arm around her shoulder.

In minutes the ambulance was there. Two men put Katie on a stretcher and carried her away. I wondered what would happen to her, what she'd tell her husband, and what Ed would tell his wife. But none of that was my problem. Police officers were talking to Ed when from his car his phone started to ring. I let it go to voicemail, but a moment later it was ringing again. This time Beth went to it and picked it up. "What do you want with him?" I heard her scream into the phone. "Can't you just leave him alone," she said. She hung up the phone and flung it into the woods.

In our room she was sitting on the edge of the bed, her face in her hands. I had not seen her this way since before the baby. "What is it, Beth?" I said. "It's going to be okay," I said. "We're okay."

She was quiet for a while. "He doesn't love her," she said at last.

I sat beside her on the bed. "I don't know, Beth," I said. "Maybe he does," I said. "He might."

"No. He doesn't," she said. "I can see it—he doesn't. It doesn't matter," she said. Her voice had changed, now. Her words were coming from far away. "You think the worst thing that'll happen is he'll break your heart," she said, "but a guy like that will scoop out everything inside of you."

Ice flashed between my temples. I looked at her. "How would you know, Beth?" I said.

Her eyes glazed over. "I just do," she said, and she stood and went to the bathroom. I heard the water for a while, then the toilet flushed. A few minutes later she came out with her face scrubbed and her pajamas on. She climbed into bed, under the covers, without saying anything. She turned her back to me and curled her knees into her chest.

"Beth," I said, "aren't you going to say anything?" There was nothing. I put my hand on her shoulder but there was no response. I shook her, light at first, then harder. Her body was limp. "Beth," I said. "What's going on?" I said. "Did something happen? Are you trying to tell me something?"

"I loved someone once," she said at last. She was quiet. "I did. I'm so sorry, but I did." She was crying now.

"Beth, what are you saying?" I said. "You don't know what you're saying now."

"It was before Rose," she said. "It didn't last long, but I did love him." She rested her head in her hands. "Now I've told you," she said, looking over at me. "I didn't think I ever would, but now I have."

Something heavy rose out of her, lingered above the bed, and settled into me. My legs felt heavy. My heart pounded in my ears. I got up and went to the bathroom. In the mirror there was a man with my face, but not me; no, it was not me. I closed my eyes and waited for it to be done, for this person to go away. Go somewhere else. Leave. Not here. Go.

When I came back to the room Beth was still. "Beth," I said. "Beth." Her eyes were opened but she did not make a sound. I knew what this was, and I braced myself for the months to come. For Rose. Then there was a flash of memory: on our honeymoon in Kauai we made snow angels on a beach of sea glass. The cool softness of the glass surprised me, and I saw Beth's old smile, heard her old laugh rise above the sound of the waves. "What did he do to you?" I said.

"I just want to go home," she said. "Please."

"Beth," I said.

I moved beside her on the bed and held her close. When her body finally softened, I looked out the window into the woods. I wondered if deer in the night get cold and lonely. I thought of Katie's husband, then, imagined what he was doing. Was he happy? Did he think *they* were happy? You settle for so many things. You make so many compromises along the way that you cannot even remember what it was you actually wanted. You can almost see the outline of it in the things you have. But only almost. And you think, *Okay, well, this is my life. It's good enough, and I can make the most of it.* Until you find out that what you thought was your life was just someone else's good acting.

Beth was asleep now, I could hear her breathing, the wild sound of her living stirring the night as she dreamed.

THE FATHER

On the first Sunday of the month their mother would drive them to the father's apartment where they would have dinner. The father was a tall, thin man with green eyes and rust-colored hair, and when he'd open the door the sweet smell of his cigar would make their noses sting. They'd go to the corner store and buy a jar of sauce, a box of spaghetti, and later, they would lick the butter from the bread to cool the spices that burned their tongues.

One time, just as they were sitting down to eat, there was a knock on the kitchen door. It was winter and already dark. On the wall over the table the father had a string of colored lights in the shape of a Christmas tree. He opened the door but before anyone spoke he said he wasn't interested.

The man peeked his red face in and waved. He said, "I see you have kids. Do you know how far ahead of things these books will put them?"

"I'm not interested," the father said.

"If you want them to go to college, you—"

The father tried to shut the door.

"Hold on," the man said, "volume three is free," he said. "Just three alone has twenty-one hundred articles."

"I'm not interested," the father said.

The man put his hand on the glass. "I'm not leaving here," he said, "until you tell me that you don't care about your kids."

"I don't care about my kids," the father said. And he closed the door and ate the spaghetti, and a few years later, he died, and they did not see him on the first Sunday, or on any other day, anymore.

Tell Me Something New

Their oldest daughter, Annie, had picked up the white chairs from the church and she was arranging them now in angled rows facing the trellis. She was careful, going back and fixing them twice, to make sure the lines were straight. She sprinkled pink rose petals in the aisle for a carpet. On the other side of their lawn, her sister Jane was under the tarp dressing a long table in linen and silver and china. She set a place card at each seat. It was their half-brother Bobby's wedding. An intimate gathering at their home. Not more than twenty-five people or so to attend. Immediate family and a few close friends.

Later, there would be music from a local jazz band. The deck would do as a stage. Tiny white lights were wound around the banisters and up around the trees too. If someone wanted to dance, there'd be room enough in the yard.

Annie and Jane had been waiting for their father, Richard, to come back with the flowers. They wondered what was keeping him. The sisters looked alike, with longish pale faces and dark, upturned eyes. Every few minutes, Jane, whose hair was a shade lighter, left what she was doing to see if her father's car was making its way down the road. "Oh, Daddy," she said when Richard finally pulled into the driveway. "We thought you'd never get back."

"I'll bet," he said, stepping from the car. "Placed the goddamn order over two months ago and do you know they didn't have a single gardenia when I got there?"

Annie had come around to meet him in the driveway too. The flowers were arranged in neat baskets in the back seat and she began filling her arms. She glared over her shoulder at her father. "You did call to confirm?" she said.

Richard's face warmed. "Well, no," he said. He wiped his hands on his pants as Annie passed them, then reached in the car and took a few baskets for Jane to carry.

"Mmmm," Jane said, inhaling the flowers. "Wonderful. Mom's favorite." And then, "So how did you get these, anyway, if they were all out?"

"Went to four different stores," Richard said. "That's how."

He filled his arms, and they made their way to the backyard. Missy Valentino, a thin young woman wearing a white shirt with a black bow tie, passed them. She was carrying a tray of sliced fruit. "Lovely day for a wedding, Mr. Cardinal," she called out with a bright smile.

"Yes," Richard called back. "Thank heavens for *that*." They had been going to the Valentino restaurant since before Missy was born; he was surprised her mother had sent her to work the wedding today instead of showing up herself.

"Mrs. Cardinal doing okay, then?"

"As well as can be expected," he said. Then in a friendlier tone he added, "Mother of the groom."

The backyard looked just as he hoped it would, but he was still troubled by Annie's sudden criticism. He tried, unsuccessfully, to shake it off. This way she had of talking to him, questioning him. If a person ordered something, where was it written that they had to call and order it all over again? The flowers *should* have been there.

He heard a sound coming from under the weeping willow tree. A young man was practicing his violin. Oh, but Jane was right. The gardenias were wonderful. Their light tropical scent seemed to lift the backyard up, carry it far away.

In Richard and Eleanor's bedroom upstairs, a steady breeze from outside made the old lace curtains move like ghosts. Richard was relieved about the weather. May in Whitesboro, New York, could have meant anything. One time, he recalled, it even snowed in May. That was the year of his graduation from Hamilton College, over forty years back. Eleanor would have never forgiven herself if the kids had their special day here, for her, only to have it ruined by something no one had any control over. This was the kind of thing that undid her, he knew well. How sometimes, a thing as simple as the weather could change the course of a day, change the course of a life, even.

He was standing in front of the antique mahogany dresser they'd bought when they were first married. "Lovely day for a wedding," she was saying as she came into the room. Someone had pinned a gardenia to her dress. It looked like wax but it was real. A touch of brown on the edges already, but he wouldn't mention it. It was the first time he'd seen her since her sisters helped her get dressed.

"Wow," he said. "Look at you," he said, falling silent, falling still. He'd felt this before—a sort of shock upon seeing his wife; he'd never been sure what she saw in him. Eleanor was a tall woman, almost seventy, with bright eyes and a mischievous smile. She was wearing a new dress. Light blue. Her best color. Her high-set cheekbones showed more now, without the weight, and the effect could be startling if you hadn't seen her in a while. But to Richard it was just a refined version of the same uncomplicated face he'd always known. It was as if she were letting him see it undressed for the first time. And he loved it more for that. When she came closer he noticed she was wearing the earrings he'd given her for their twentieth wedding anniversary. They looked like teardrops but they were crystal. He felt a pang of something—pride, he guessed; he'd never been sure if she liked them.

"Really," he said, kissing her.

Some of her lipstick came away with him. She rubbed it with her thumb.

He said, "Just stunning." Details now. Her eyes. He hadn't seen her eyes like this, all made up, in a long while. They were alive again. Looked like ice on an awakening lake. Reminded him of what he loved about her: that hint of something wild, something playful, going on beneath the surface.

"Silly man," she said, her laugh still girlish. Always shy of compliments. She squinted, and curled her bottom lip. It was her way of telling him, he understood by now, two things: he'd said the right thing, and she didn't want to ruin her makeup. He knew to stop. She moved behind him and made quick strokes at his shirt until it felt smooth. He was surprised by her strength. "Don't you know I would have been happy with 'not hideous'?" she said. She touched her choppy, beige hair.

"Tell me something new," he told the mirror. This was a question they asked each other from the start; a sort of game they'd used to get to know each other, only it had stayed. She turned to him and rested her forehead on his.

"We don't have time."

"We have a minute," he said. His hands went around her waist. If he wanted to, it seemed he could make fingers touch fingers. Ribs. Spine. Hips. And to think of all those years she spent on diets!

"Something new," she said. "Rosalie and I used to steal from Woolworths." She pulled away from him, giggling.

Richard brightened. "No," he said.

There was a glint in her eye. "It's true," she said.

"So," Richard asked, "what did you steal?"

"Makeup! We'd take turns. One of us would slip a lipstick, or rouge, what have you, up our sleeve, while the other kept an eye on the clerk."

The curtains were still moving. "I can't believe you never told me that," he said. Then, "Did you get caught?"

"Come on," she said. "Me?" She took a silk scarf from the box on the dresser. "Could you give me a hand with this?" She turned her back to him.

The scarf was pretty, with lots of colors. Richard recognized the pattern though he didn't know the name for it, or even if there was a name for it. He took it from her hand and went about wrapping it on her head the way he knew she liked it. "It's very pretty," he told her as he worked the silk around her head.

She watched in the mirror.

"I can't believe you never told me that," he said again.

She caught his eye in the mirror just as he finished with the scarf. "See that?" she said. "You're learning."

It occurred to him then—this was what everyone would see.

Outside, the sun was dropping in the afternoon sky, and in this light Bobby's hair was fiery in the way Eleanor's had been before the kids. He was standing underneath the trellis with Pastor Pat when she and Richard made their way down the aisle. The violinist was playing something that sounded vaguely familiar to Richard. He'd never liked classical music, but in recent months Eleanor enjoyed listening to it, said it soothed her, and, he supposed, it soothed him too. They took their seats in the front row and turned to see Annie and Jane walk down the aisle one by one.

When Renee, the bride, appeared at the end of the aisle arm in arm with her father, everyone rose.

Six months ago when Bobby called to say he'd gotten engaged, Eleanor hadn't been diagnosed yet. It was a cold December afternoon, the fire was going, they were setting up the tree.

Richard had wound the thick pins into the bottom of the trunk, and his hands were sticky with sap and the smell of pine. Someone said once that sugar made the tree stay longer, and he used it now every time in the watering can, though he didn't know if it was true or not.

The branches had settled to where they would end up.

They were passing a string of colored lights around the tree to each other. After a time, Eleanor asked, "Do you think she's right for him?"

"Yes," Richard said.

"I just get the feeling he's scared of her sometimes," she said. "So bossy." She was adjusting the lights in the front of the tree. *"Bobby, can you get me a glass of water? Bobby, can you run to the store? Bobby, can you—"*

"Now, Mama—"

"Doesn't cook," she said, handing Richard the bundle. In a minute she sighed. "I suppose we'll all have to fly out to California for the wedding," she said. She worked quietly for a while adjusting the lights, then said, "I'll bet she *made* him propose."

"Made him propose?"

"Oh, forget it." She took several steps back. "Right there," she said, pointing her finger. "Do you see that?"

"Where?" Richard asked. "Here?"

She nodded and he made the adjustments. When she went for the ornaments he knew he'd done it right. The first one she picked was old, one of Richard's favorites, had been his mother's. If you set it over a light, the heat made the tiny figures on the inside twirl.

She went on. "You'd have to be a woman to understand," she said. "Anyway, he did say they'd have a long engagement."

Waiting for a wedding day is the longest wait in a person's life. At least, this was what Richard used to think. It was that way for Eleanor. She certainly was in a rush to marry him, he remembered. And what a bride she made.

Her face behind that veil; he still saw it sometimes when he blinked.

His heart had felt this same way—it *started*—when he saw her for the first time at his hardware store. He heard the bells on the door twinkle. Looked up. Saw her. So *that's what his life until now had been about.* Bobby was there, in his stroller, crying. He waited. No husband came. He jingled his car keys for the boy.

She said, "You're giving him your car?" That hint of irony. "What a nice man you must be." *No wedding ring.*

"Every little boy needs a car," Richard said. Women like Eleanor didn't talk to him. In an ordinary world, the boy's father would have been there to quiet him when he cried. But, Richard would soon learn, that man had been lost, two years earlier in a car accident on his way home from a night shift at the hospital. Now Eleanor was taking the time to charm him, and he was charmed.

He asked her once what it was like, losing her first husband.

"What did you do when you found out?"

"I wanted to die," he remembered her saying. She told him that when she got the call she ran straight for the balcony. But when she got to the very edge, she remembered something about heaven, how doing it meant she would never see him again.

"You must have really loved him," he said. *You must have really loved him,* he thought.

Sitting here, now, he hated to think of everyone's greedy eyes on his wife. He hated to think about the whispering, the gossip. About what they'd say after. He hated to think about the pity. Eleanor was too good for pity. Even now, like this. In the paper, he could see it now, what they'd write: *Dear wife of Richard; dear mother of Robert, Anne, and Jane; dear Sister of Gloria and Eva. A simple woman with a kind and gentle nature. Revered throughout her family for her special holiday recipes.*

Oh, how easy to sum a person up. To be summed up. At the grocery store too, near the vegetables and the slabs of raw beef. They'd say it quickly, move on to other things, he knew. This was how people relayed information to one another. This was how people told each other bad things. With some joy in it. Always with a bit of joy. They'd make her sound heroic to absolve their guilt. Would say something like, "She put up a courageous fight, but she lost her battle." The gall they had to put it this way. Her battle. As if she ever had a fighting chance. The carnage. It made him enraged to think about the news making its way through her chubby-faced bridge buddies in their flowery skirts who hadn't been by to see her since. Her sister, who never even *called* anymore. Even their own daughters, who did only the bare minimum. Richard knew it now in a way he hadn't before: the entire world was made of cowards.

Eleanor begged him not to say anything now or after, reminding him that everyone copes in their own way. "Just because you're losing the same person," she'd said, "doesn't mean you're losing the same thing."

The first few months after the doctors told Eleanor that it was stage 4, liver, she would wake up terrified. "Do I have cancer? Do I have cancer?" she screamed. Richard had no choice but to answer. He had no choice but to say yes, and each time it was as if she had never heard it before.

During the day she held it together. She made prearrangements. Plans, lists, calls. It reminded Richard of when she was planning their wedding day. Asking again which scriptures should be read, what she should wear. She picked her blue dress and a necklace that had once belonged to her mother. *We're too young for this,* Richard wanted to tell her. *We're not ready for this,* he wanted to say.

"With this ring I thee *dread*," she whispered in his ear just before the couple exchanged their vows. It was her joke at every wedding since he could remember. He'd been waiting for it. He caught her eye and they laughed.

Bobby told Renee he was going to love her through good times and bad, through richer and poorer, through sickness and health, for all the days of his life. Renee said the same things to him. Richard tried to keep himself from thinking it, but one thought kept going through his mind: *Is that all?*

As the new couple floated into the applause, Eleanor wept. Handing her a handkerchief, Richard asked, "Are you okay?"

Her eyes stayed on her son. "My God," she said, stunned. "He looks exactly like his father did."

After dinner, and after the jazz band played for a while, Renee floated over to the table, her white dress glowing in the night. Annie and Jane both stood up when she neared. The women talked for a few minutes, laughing and glancing over at one of the groomsmen, then Renee bent down so that she and Eleanor were eye level. "Mom," she said, "I'd really like it if you and Bobby had the next dance."

Eleanor looked at Richard. He nodded.

"Oh," Eleanor said. "That's kind of you."

Bobby appeared a moment later and took his mother's hand, and Richard heard Eleanor tell him as they drifted off, "Your father would have been so proud."

His father. Not Richard. Richard was not his father. Not his *real* father. And no one ever got that confused anymore now that the boy was grown. They couldn't have been more different, really. Richard was short. Shorter than Eleanor by at least an inch, something he'd always hated. And God help him if he could ever get that dumb, *Yes, sir; good day, ma'am* smirk off his face whenever he saw any person. Always wanting to please. Always wanting to be liked. Save for a puff of white hair over each of his ears, his head was bald. His scalp shone—glistened when there was sun. Had been this way since he was in his thirties. What's more, there was a raised scar about four inches over his right eyebrow from a bike accident he had as a kid. He knew it caught everyone's eye when they talked to him. He could see their eyes not look at it. Over the years he'd done what he could to lose weight, but every time he lost five pounds, he'd gain seven back.

And Bobby. He loved the boy as if he were his own son. But his own son he was not. Handsome, like his father. Strong in ways Richard was not. Strong in ways that had to do with your guts. With what went on inside. With what you did when no one was watching. So this was it. Here it was. He was seeing it now for the first time. Her first love. Her first choice. They were dancing together in the moonlight. And this was how she looked with "her Bob." Through the years, she'd taken to calling him "my Bob" to make it clear when she was talking about the father, and not the son. So Richard did it eventually too. "Your Bob," he'd heard himself say more than a time or two. And now from this distance, he could see it; he finally knew how it looked to see her the way she once was, the way she should have always been.

A long, lonely drone. A deep, sad whine from the violin. It had started to rain. Thunder rumbled in the near distance. Raindrops slapped the pavement. Eleanor and Bobby kept dancing anyway. Under the weeping willow tree the violinist pointed his instrument in their direction as they moved around the yard, the vibrato adding shimmer to their dance. Each turn lighting for Richard the life that could have been. Near the pine he saw his wife and her Bob, their children, spinning, hand in hand. He could hear the children's laughter over the violin, over the rain. Beside the tarp, their home. A small cottage, like the ones Eleanor had always pointed out. She was older now, and her hair had come back in long and thick and white, and she was working in her garden. In their bedroom, Bob caressed her bare shoulder.

The voice of her whispers sent a chill through Richard's spine. Springtime birds heard it too. The tiny white lights sparkled on up through the trees to the sky like stars, and in the darkness her dress glowed white and it could have been her wedding day. So lively and peaceful and beautiful, she could have been the bride. And as Eleanor rested her head on his chest, and he held her close and danced her one last graceful time around the yard to the music of everyone's applause, a sudden burst of pain ran through Richard's heart, and he knew then: she never loved him the way she loved her Bob.

In bed that night, the sound of the crickets from outside got Richard thinking of summers he'd spent at the lake when he was a kid. He and his younger brother loved to swing from a rope and then drop down into the deep water, catch fish to throw back in. When it was dark they'd pull night crawlers out of the cool earth, store them in old coffee cans with air holes cut in the lid. He was thinking about how nothing else smelled as clean as dirt when the scent of her lavender lotion brought her back to him.

"Are you awake?" he said.

There was a movement in the bed, and the shadow of her face. "She called me Mom," Eleanor said.

"And?"

"Well, I wish I could say I'll learn to live with it."

"That's not funny."

She matched the tips of her fingers to the tips of his fingers. "She'll take care of him?"

"She'll take care of him."

After a moment, "Tell me something new," she said.

"Something new," he said. He cleared his throat. "Something new." His mind went to faraway things. Near things. Impossible things. What was there that she hadn't given to him, been to him? What was there left that he hadn't told her? This graceful woman. Flashes of memory. His favorite things. His first things. People. People. So many people had come into his life, gone out of his life. And what was there that she didn't already know?

"Did I ever tell you anything about a rabbit?" he said at last.

"Rabbit?" she asked. "I don't think so."

"My brother and I found it in the woods," he said. "It was hurt—its leg, I think. We took care of it for a few months. When it was better, we let it back out into the woods." It might not have seemed like much of a story, but he felt unsteady inside thinking about it, even now.

She leaned close and held him.

He thought of all the new things he would never have the chance to tell her. "How do you picture heaven?" he asked her.

"Stop," she said.

"No," he said, "I want to know." He'd always let her go to church alone.

"Just someplace pretty, I guess." She said, "Lots of grass and bright flowers. Trees and lakes and sun." She laughed a little. "That must sound silly to you," she said.

"Do you picture houses?"

"Not really," she said.

A thought came to Richard from far back that had to do with place cards like he used to make in school. He was wondering if the angels cut up white cards, and write your name in glue, and then sprinkle gold glitter over it. "In my mind it's something like a fancy wedding, I guess," he said. He rubbed his forehead. "Big round tables with linen tablecloths. I can see my grandparents and mom and dad sitting at one. My brother. I picture them all just sitting there together, with their eyes and their champagne glasses sparkling." He thought of place cards again, wondered about husbands and wives.

"And me," she said.

He knew her face well, and his eyes had adjusted to the darker light. "And you," he said, without turning away from her.

We're Not So Far from There

My wife has this friend she used to go with. They were high school sweethearts, and then broke it off just after he went to school in New York City. Charles was the one who ended it. She told me all about it. He'd said he needed to be free for a while, make something of himself. It was that kind of thing. Maybe someday it would be the right time for them, he had told her, but right now it wasn't the right time. She took it hard, my wife. She'd already given it up to him. She was not herself for a long time after—her mother told me this part.

But through the years they kept up communication and managed to stay friends. Even after we got married. He's an actor now. Or, what I should say, trying to be. Sometimes when we're watching TV at night, a commercial will come on and flash his face. Every time it's that same "I had her first" smile.

When he calls she goes in the back room. Sometimes she gets to laughing so loud I can't hear the television. I usually just go for a walk.

Last week after they talked she came out of the room and put her eyes on the TV, but she wasn't watching anything, I could tell. When the commercials came on, her face didn't change.

"What's wrong?" I asked.

She stayed quiet. I watched the commercials. "Charles got married this week," she said finally.

"Oh, did he?" I said. "I didn't know he was seeing anyone, even." I tried to hold back from smiling.

"No, me neither. He's only known her for a few months. Went to Vegas," she said. "Figured he'd make it real before he lost his nerve."

"Sounds familiar," I said.

"They're coming to town next weekend," she said. "He wants to tell his family in person."

I went and got us two Coronas. I put hers on the table in front of her and then took a cigarette from her pack and lit it. "You seem sad," I said, and sat back down.

"Sad?" she said. "No—I don't know what it is. It's just weird, you know?" She was scratching the back of her neck and looking at the carpet.

"I guess."

"I told him we'd have to get together, the four of us, to celebrate." She looked around the apartment. No lights were on. Just the TV. "You'll have to fix that wallpaper in the kitchen, okay, and get your hair cut."

"Okay," I said. "No problem."

"And I'd like us to go out for a change. I'd like to take them someplace special. As their gift," she said. She walked over to her purse, took out her wallet, and started to count her cash.

"What are you doing?" I said.

"I told you," she said. "I want to take them someplace nice, and I want us to pay for the whole thing as a gift. I told them we'd take them out to celebrate."

"Deb," I said. "You know I'd love to do that. You know I wish we could do that, but it's not a good time right now," I said. "We have to cut back on things, not the opposite. Besides, do you really think Mr. Hollywood needs us to pay the bill?" I took a sip of my beer. I looked at the TV. She knew the score. I'd been out of work for six months and her job at the restaurant was hardly going to leave us room for extras like this.

"Maybe it'd be better if you cooked anyway," I said. "You could do up that roasted chicken with the gravy and the potatoes. It's better than any restaurant food anyway." She liked to hear that sort of thing about her cooking.

Debbie put her face in her hands. She didn't say anything.

"What is it?" I said.

She didn't answer. She walked into the bathroom and closed the door. She stayed in there for a while with the water running. I couldn't hear anything. I turned the TV back on, but my show had gone off. I changed the channels. The news was on over and over again. They were talking about that goddamned arsonist again. Someone had been setting houses on fire over in Cornhill. They had set another one just now. This made eight. The houses were close together over there, and the fires would catch. Once it got started, there was no stopping it. Entire blocks were going up in flames. People were getting hurt. Two had died. The families were living in shelters, but the shelters were overcrowded with children. Someone brought cots to the school, and people were sleeping there at night now, in the cafeteria.

It was a crisis. The people needed clothing, food, homes, and medical care. The reporters were asking everyone to give fifty dollars. We had put our fifty aside and we were waiting for someone to come by and collect it. The arsonist left no clues; they had no leads. The police patrolling the neighborhoods saw nothing, and then bam, another house would go up. There were rumors. People were talking. They were saying that the police were starting the fires themselves, to burn the crack up from the inside, so that they could take the neighborhood down and then rebuild it. That was the only way to do it once things had gone so far—to start from scratch. It was what people were saying, but I didn't believe it for a minute. It was crazy talk.

Debbie had been in the bathroom for a time and I thought I'd better check things out. I knocked on the door and called to her but she didn't answer. I tried the knob but it was locked, so I grabbed a butter knife from the kitchen and undid it. I opened the door and saw her standing in front of the mirror with a tweezers, pulling away at some white hairs on the top of her head. Her makeup was off; she had been crying; but she was finished up with it now, I could tell. Our eyes met in the mirror, but neither one of us said anything. I started at a red bump that was swelling on the side of my nose. "The arsonist struck again," I said.

"Christ," she said. "Again?"

"Yep. And no one saw a thing."

"This makes eight?" she said.

"Eight," I said.

"Christ," she said again. "We're not so far from there. Pretty soon they'll be burning things up over here."

"I don't think so," I said. "I don't think you need to worry about that." I finished up with the pimple and leaned against the sink. I looked at her, but she kept on with what she was doing. "What is it, Debbie?" I said, putting my hand on her shoulder. "Is this about dinner? Is that what? We'll figure it out. We have that fifty dollars we'd set aside, and there's at least that much in the bank."

"It's not dinner," she said.

"What then?"

"I don't know, really," she said. She put the tweezers down. "I'm scared. I've been feeling scared for a long time, and I don't know what it is."

"What is it? What are you afraid of, Debbie?" I said, and leaned in to her. "We'll get through this. I'll find another job. It won't be long now."

"Is this what you pictured when you were younger—like when you were eighteen? Did you think your life would be this way?"

"I don't know what I thought," I said. "I suppose I pictured it something like this. Things aren't so bad. I've got you. We've got our home. It's not so bad. Is it?"

She didn't answer me.

"Someday we're gonna—"

"Don't," she said. "*Someday* means *never*."

Something inside of me got hot when she said that. "This is about Charles, isn't it?" I said.

"Jesus," she said. "Not everything is about Charles."

"Oh, come on," I said. "You do this whenever he calls. You get all shaken up and you don't look at me for a week. You think I can't tell when you're thinking about Prince Charles?" Something came over me. All through their first time she said they held hands. "Well, guess what," I said. And this was a thing I'd been wanting to say to her since the day I met her. "He ain't comin' back for you, lady," I said. And when I said this, I moved in toward her real close so that my face was right in front of her.

She didn't say anything. Just kept looking at me. It felt like something. I could tell something was about to happen here, something was about to change. Something was on the tip of her tongue and she couldn't say it. For a long time, she couldn't say it.

THANKSGIVING

The last time I saw my brother, Paul, was on the day before Thanksgiving. It was cold, even for November in Watertown, and the radiators gave a thunderous rattle every time they went on in my mother's little three bedroom apartment. The insulation was never what it should have been in my childhood home, and there were always icy drafts. We wore heavy sweaters.

My sister, Kristen, my mother, and I didn't spend much time together anymore. As kids, Kristen and I shared each other's clothes and were each other's best friends. Now she was thirty-two and I was twenty-eight, and we had lives of our own. But there's a closeness that comes from starting in the same place, and that closeness felt tangible when we were all there together.

For my mother's sake, we said we would forgive him. It was the year she almost died. Not from the heart attacks but from the complications that had to do with the bypass surgery. Having her whole family in one place had taken on a new importance to her. There was something else that mattered more now too: I wanted to see her happy.

On Wednesday evening, just as the light outside changed so that the snow looked lavender, I heard my brother's heavy steps on the porch stairs, recalling for me the heeled boots he used to wear, and then I heard the doorbell ring. I picked up my mother's small poodle, Snowball, so she wouldn't run outside into the cold night when my mother opened the door. My mother still carried extra weight from before her heart attacks, and she needed a cane, now, to get around, but we let her go to the door anyway; she had kept up some basic contact with my brother over the past ten years, and we hadn't. I was standing in front of the plaid loveseat. Kristen was sitting across from me on the old blue velour couch that my mother still had from when we were kids. She was braiding her daughter Sadie's red hair, while Sadie kept her freckled face tucked in a book. Sadie was wearing a sweater that looked too big for her, and this made her seem defenseless and small. It was the first time she was meeting her uncle, a person she'd never heard us talk much about.

Years ago my mother used a number two pencil to sketch a picture of Jesus on the back of a pizza box. There are oil spots up in the corner, but it was framed now and hung over her TV, just past the front door. A crucifixion image—a close-up, just, of Jesus's wounded face. My eyes fell on it as she opened the door; a gust of frigid outside air swept in through the living room, and the radiator clanked noisily on. I thought of my brother as I remembered him—someone who, seething, once stabbed a butcher knife through a locked door that I was hiding behind.

My brother came in and my mother's body blocked the doorway. She opened her arms to welcome him. I knew she still loved him—*her prince*, she used to call him. *Her only son. Her firstborn.*

He let himself fall into her embrace a bit, but his arms stayed stiff at his sides. The hair that used to be blond was mostly gray now. He had thirteen years on me, the baby, so I don't know why this particular change surprised me as it did. Right away I noticed a sort of tremor he had going in his neck; it wasn't anything I'd noticed a person doing before. Almost like a chicken's neck, it moved. He was dressed well, and this took me by surprise too. He had on a tweed blazer that looked expensive and a pair of dark slacks with well-set pleats. Someone had ironed them. The shoes he wore were the kind of shoes businessmen wear with little leather tassels right there in the middle.

"All right, now," he said, in a peculiar voice that had picked up unmistakable hints of Kentucky, where he'd been living all these years. He squeezed past our mother, his palms facing her in apparent surrender. His eyes darted between my sister and me, but there was only a vague look of recognition on his aged face. Kristen and I looked very much alike: the same long blond hair, the same medium height and frame, the same pointy features. We smiled at him. We were there, and we meant to be generous about it—forgiving.

"Go about your business now," he went, his chicken neck and his Kentucky going ever so slightly, and then, "Show's over here," he added, fanning his hands as if there were insects buzzing in his direct vicinity. As he walked off, looking at nothing in particular, a wicked-looking smile seized his face. I noticed his smell, just like it used to be, musk and cigarettes, and something else too—his nose was bigger than I remembered. It was a sharp and crooked-looking thing that seemed to come apart and change directions midway. He went on through the kitchen and into the bathroom, shutting the door and fussing with the lock, testing it a few times to make sure.

I set Snowball down and she followed quickly after him, letting out a few half-hearted barks at the door. My mother had found her years before out on the street and took her in and nursed her to health on a diet of oatmeal and milk until she was able to keep down dog food. She let Snowball sleep beside her in her own warm bed. Because of this, the dog had a protective nature now. She didn't like it when new people came around—didn't like loud noises or sudden moves. My sister and I glanced at each other for an awkward moment. We followed our mother, who, I could see, looked overwhelmed, and had started to cry.

"Don't worry, Mom," I told her. "It's just been a long time—that's all," I said. She didn't say anything except to excuse herself to her bedroom, which was right off the kitchen.

My sister and Sadie and I sat down around the old round Formica table in the kitchen. The kitchen was good-sized for apartments in this area, and so it fit a good-sized table. It was a cheery enough room—the top half covered in faded wallpaper that had tiny yellow flowers, the bottom painted in that same soft yellow; and I liked sitting there at that table. As a young girl I sat there after school and watched my mother as she cooked dinner, listening to her tell the far-off stories from her childhood. The bathroom was off the kitchen, and we knew that whatever we said, my brother would be able to hear, so, sitting there now, we knew to stay quiet. Anyway, what was there to say? Here was our brother—come back—an old man now. His hair was gray and he wore some gray hair on his face too. His thin, boyish body had filled out into something sturdy. He'd become distinguished-looking, handsome. He could have been a doctor. Except, we knew he was a bank teller and not a doctor.

Sadie said, "That's not how I pictured him."

Kristen put her finger to her lips, and I said, "Me either."

It was a while before my brother came out of the bathroom. When he finally did, he seemed more at ease, and he set his tweed jacket carefully over the back of the chair at the head of the table, opposite where Sadie was sitting. He opened the refrigerator. Glass clanked as he moved his hands inside. "No wine," he muttered, reaching instead for a bottle of beer, twisting off the gold cap with the bottom of his shirt. He sat down where his coat was, and my mother came back into the kitchen then, and she sat down next to him in a seat near the wall beside Kristen. She had fixed her face with makeup and changed into the red sweater that she'd worn last Christmas. I sat down across from where my mother and Kristen were sitting.

"So tell us about the drive," my mother said, "and how's Kentucky?" she added with a smile, tapping his hand gently with her own.

"The drive was a drive," he said, sliding his hand away. He added, "And Kentucky is Kentucky." His eyes darted around the table. My mother's face flushed. She was quiet. Then she said, gesturing, "Of course you remember Kristen," and then, "and this beauty here—her daughter, Sadie. She'll be eleven next month."

My brother got a dumb look on his face and focused on Sadie with his lips parted as if it were the first time he'd noticed she was there. He tipped his head off to the side as though he was trying to hear a distant sound. Sadie's smile faded under his stare. Her freckled face got blotchy and red. She looked down at Snowball, who had been wiggling at her feet. My mother went on with what she was saying. She was talking faster, and it was plain to see that she was flustered. "And of course," she said, reaching over the table and squeezing my hand, "my Robyn."

My brother said, "Yes. Good. Good." He said, "My sisters, I think I can remember my baby sisters, for Christ's sake." He shot a fierce look at my mother. Then there was his odd smile again, and it wasn't clear from his look if he was thinking of something that brought him joy or caused him pain; he looked again at Sadie. She was scratching at Snowball's head now and saying things to the little dog in her sweet voice.

My brother reached into his pocket, took out his wallet, and removed a crisp twenty-dollar bill. He extended his arm over the table with a kind-eyed smile and said, "Here you go. Have your mommy get you a toy."

Sadie looked at her mother for a show of approval and then took the money in her hand. Her face lit up as she folded the bill and stuffed it into the pocket of her purple pants. She was quiet, but the color stayed on her face for a time.

I went to the stove and turned off the flame. The soup was ready, I could tell from the smell, and the boiling broth was causing the windows to get steamy. I took the ladle from the wall where it hung next to the other utensils and scooped the soup into bowls. I put the first bowl down in front of my brother. "Here you go," I said. It was the first thing I'd said to him in ten years.

"Should warm you up," my mother said proudly, adding, "I made it just the way you like it, with tiny meatballs and tortellini."

I noticed him squinting at the bowl as I served the soup to the others. He said, "How you'd remember a thing like that is beyond me." Then, without waiting, he took his spoon and started eating. He made slurping sounds as he ate it. As I sat down, I saw that Sadie was having herself a giggle about this. My eyes met hers and there was a moment of mutual understanding. Some broth had started a thin stream down his beard, and if he noticed this, it didn't bother him enough for him to use his napkin. Without saying anything, Sadie walked over and handed him the basket of fresh Italian bread. I could see that she was coming out of herself, and this pleased me.

"Oh, and the butter, Sadie-girl," he said playfully, and with a full smile that revealed his mouthful of jagged teeth. "Can you get me the butter too, sweet girl?" She did and sat back down. "So tell me, what grade are you in?"

"Fifth," she said. She moved her spoon around the bowl and found herself a tiny meatball. Sadie was a serious girl and didn't have many friends: after school she preferred reading to watching TV.

"Do you still paint?" I interrupted. There were only a few things I knew about him: that he liked to paint landscapes, and that he was very good at it, was one. "I just got a new watercolor set," I went on. "I'll bring it out later," and then, "Maybe you could show me some tricks."

"There's not really any tricks," he said. But after a minute he seemed to reconsider. He said, "Here's a tip—divide your paper into three parts—what you're painting, the subject, that shouldn't be in the middle part. But you probably know that much already, right?" he said, adding, "And keep your horizons high or low. Things like that."

"Interesting," I said. It was something I didn't know. "That's great—I'll be sure to keep it in mind." I felt funny talking to him like this, as if there were nothing between us, as if we were just any two ordinary people whose histories were not mangled in this complicated way. And there was a pang of sadness too, and I wondered if this was what it was like to have an older brother. Someone there ahead of you to clear the path and tell you the little things that are hard to learn but easy to know.

"Just basic stuff," he mumbled, recovering himself. "If you're really interested in painting, you should take a class. They'd tell you that and more on the first day." He stood up and helped himself to another beer. Then he went to the stove and filled his bowl with more soup. Snowball was circling the table and sniffing the floor, waiting for something to fall. My brother sat back down and watched her as he took sips from his new beer. "That the same dog?" he asked finally.

"No," I said, giving Snowball a look that got her tail going. "Looks like her, but that was a long time ago."

My brother rubbed the dented side of his nose and looked back at Sadie. "So I bet you've got yourself a little boyfriend at school? I'm guessing you've had your first kiss already," he said, buttering a piece of bread and then soaking up the broth with it. He ripped the tough crust with his teeth and swallowed hard. His chicken neck picked up. "That right?" he asked, with a tilt of his head. "Have you been up in a tree yet?" adding, "K-I-S-S-I-N-G."

Kristen straightened up in her seat. She put her spoon down and gave my mother a serious look. But my mother did not look up. She just kept going with her soup.

"No," Sadie said.

"She's too young for boys," Kristen said, resting her hand on her daughter's shoulder. After a moment she relaxed. "I've got a few more years before I have to start worrying about that," she said. "Thank God."

My brother leaned back in his chair. His knees fell apart and he cocked his head. "Oh," he said. "You can't believe that now, can you?" he said. "Kids these days. They start young. I bet little Sadie here has got herself a boyfriend and she just hasn't told you about him. Ain't that right, sweet girl?" he asked, turning to Sadie with a smile.

Sadie's face mottled. She giggled a bit, covering her mouth. "No," she said. But this time, it was less convincing.

My mother smiled in her granddaughter's direction. "Oh," she said. "She's still a baby," she said. "She has friends that are girls, and friends that are boys." She looked at her soup for a moment, and then she raised her eyes on my brother. Something savage happened to his face, then; we both saw it. My mother turned away from him at once. There was panic in her eyes when she next looked at me.

I said, "What about you? Are you seeing anyone?"

But he kept his eyes fixed on my mother.

She turned her face down, the way she always used to when he'd start with one of his rants.

"A baby?" my brother said at last. "I'd hardly call *that* a baby," he said. He got a cigarette from his jacket pocket and rolled it with his fingers before lighting it up, and then he took a few long, hard drags from it, went to the kitchen sink, ran water on it, and tossed it in the garbage. He came back to the table and sat down. He turned to Sadie and said, "She's got tweets, for Christ's sake," he said, laughing. "I never saw a baby with tweeters," he said.

"That's enough," Kristen said, standing. "I'm not going to sit here and—"

"I bet her boyfriend's seen those tweeters too," my brother interrupted. He went on, "I bet he's kissed those sweet pink rosebuds," he said.

Sadie was breathing hard and crying now. She stood up. "Shut up," she shouted, covering her chest as best she could with her skinny arms. Kristen came around and rubbed her head, but it didn't calm her. She tried to take the girl away, but Sadie wriggled from her.

"Tweets, tweets," he said, again and again, throwing his head back to show the jagged teeth that crowded his mouth.

"Shut up!" Sadie yelled again. She was red-faced and breathing hard and the more she cried out for him to stop, the more my brother cackled and did it anyway.

She shouted it out with her mouth wide open. "Beak!" she said, and then again, "Beak! Beak!" she screamed at him. I looked at her, confused, but when she gestured toward her nose I understood what she meant. The yelling seemed to have a calming effect on her, and she stopped crying. She squinted. "That's right," she said. "You look like a bird with that big old ugly nose on your face," and then she said again, with a bit of song in her voice, "Bee-eeak!" And when he stopped smiling, she seemed more confident. "Beak! Beak! Beak," she said. She was so proud.

"Sweet girl," he said in a serious voice, "don't you say that again," adding, "do you hear what I'm telling you?" He sat still but his upper lip quivered. "Do you understand what I'm saying?" His neck moved freely now, but his eyes stayed fierce.

She was silent for a moment, just looking at him, but then there was a tiny smirk that betrayed her. "Beak!" she said again, this time with a peep of her own sweet laughter; she covered her mouth as though she thought they were playing a sort of game. But when he pounced over the table to get her, and when the dishes flew out from under him and shattered, and Snowball barked, and my brother growled and snapped out into the air, her innocent expression changed into one of terror, and she flew under the table and onto her hands and knees where she crawled around until she found my trembling legs and clung and squeezed and whimpered.

"You think you're gonna hide under your aunt's skirt now, do you?" he said, rushing over to where she was, shedding blood from the hand he'd sliced on a broken bowl.

I tried to shield her, but there was no way to hold him back. My brother yanked her from her hiding spot, and pulled his arm up behind his head and slapped her freckled face with all his animal force. And then he did it again right there on the same cheek, this time making the sound come louder, this time leaving a streak of his own bright blood on her skin. And when he was finished she opened her mouth to scream but no sound came. Until it did. Until she made her shrill piercing sound and covered her welted face with her hands and ran clumsily to the bathroom, her mother stumbling after her.

Outside, the wind had picked up and was making whistling noises as it chased itself around in circles, futilely, like a dog going after its tail. My mother did not let him stay for Thanksgiving. And when she willfully and forcefully pushed closed the door behind him against that icy wind, I understood that hers was the heaviest door I'd ever seen, and that if I tried for one thousand years I would never know what it was like to have my hand there on that cold steel knob. And that was when I finally forgave her.

EVERYTHING THAT'S LEFT

Matthew's wife was upstate for the weekend, with their son, visiting her relatives. She'd be home again tomorrow; the boy was going to stay behind for a vacation. Matthew had just finished up in his bedroom with Angie. After a long talk under the covers, they decided that the best thing for everyone would be for him to leave tonight. Angie had been wishing this for a while now, though she'd never asked for it straight out.

Right away he started to fill some suitcases with the things that were his. The things that were his would fit into one bag, maybe two, he figured. Clothes, razors, paperbacks—things like that. Everything else belonged to his wife, and he knew it. She had paid for all the furniture, along with the television, the stereo, and all the art they had hanging on the walls. She had paid for the pots and pans and for the car too. There was no point in disputing any of it. The child was a thing that belonged to him too, but that was something he didn't mind his wife keeping.

Matthew was finished with his bags and was having a last look around the apartment to check for things he might have missed. Angie watched as he made his way in and out of the bedroom. She was leaning against the brick wall over in the corner, winding a bit of her long black hair around her finger. Matthew walked up to her and put his hands on her shoulders. He said, "How about a smile? Isn't that something you can do for me?"

But Angie didn't smile. She walked to the other side of the room and sat down at a table where some of his wife's makeup was still laid about. She looked in the mirror and moved things on the table. She picked up a tube of lipstick, opened it, and pressed it over her lips.

She said, "I don't know, Matthew. Don't get me wrong, you know I'm all for you leaving." She was quiet for a moment. "It's just—do you really think a note is the best way?" She was looking in the mirror again, wiping the smeared makeup from underneath her eyes. "I mean, it's not like we're in high school. There's a kid in the picture, for Christ's sake. Can't you tell her to her face?"

Matthew sat on the bed and put his head in his hands. "What are you trying to do here?" he said. He ran his fingers through his graying hair. "Look, I know it's not something people do every day, a letter and all, but if it's going to happen, it's got to be this way. It's this or nothing." He thought of the times when he'd tried to tell his wife. There were many times. The words would play over and over again in his mind. He couldn't say them. This was really none of Angie's business anyway. Not this part. If he wanted to do it with a letter, goddamn it, that's what he'd do. He said, "It's not like it's out of the blue or something. It's not like she doesn't know there's a problem." He moved the bags onto the floor and stood up. He yanked at the covers on the bed. "Help me with this, would you?" he said. "Grab that end."

Angie pulled at the sheets and the blankets. "Of course, Matthew. Of course there's something wrong here. She'd have to be blind not to know. It's just a matter of decency, that's all. People are going to ask. People will want to know how. They'll talk. It'll mean something."

She shook the bottom sheet hard and then tucked it in its place. She pulled the top sheet tight and lifted a piece from the bottom corner, tucked in what was hanging out. She walked around and did the same thing on Matthew's side. They both shifted the comforter into place, and Angie tugged at it here and there until the pattern was set right.

Matthew said, "It's not like that. My wife doesn't worry about what people think. She's not like you."

"What's that supposed to mean?" Angie said, her voice high. "You make it sound like I'm some kind of—"

"You don't know my wife. That's all," Matthew said.

"Jesus. Do you hear yourself? You say it like she's better than me."

"Look," he said. He was talking loud now. "I know my wife. I know her better than anyone knows her. I know what will hurt her. I know what she needs and what she doesn't need."

"Fine," Angie said. "I won't worry about it then." She walked back to the table and sat down. It was clear something Matthew had said was cutting things up inside her.

Matthew picked up some paper and a pen from the table. He walked toward the kitchen. "Just give me a few minutes," he said.

When he got to the kitchen he sat down at the table and looked at the blank paper. He thought about the things he'd wanted to say. He wanted to make the letter clear, so there wouldn't be things left to wonder about. He thought he could start at the beginning. He could tell her about how they had rushed into things, because of the baby. He could tell her how he felt when the baby came: those thoughts that had to do with swallowing pills. But how could he explain that in a few lines? What could he say to explain that? He thought that maybe, first, he could get into how he was only twenty-three, and how he'd never wanted any of it. He could tell her about his dreams. He had dreams then. There were things he wanted to be. Things he was going to do. He was going to finish school. He thought maybe it would be good to tell her about the dreams here, so that she'd understand. He could tell her how he wanted to get out of there. Tell her how he hated that town and every single thing in it. Tell her how he hated his job at the factory, and that every time he walked through the door he told himself he was doing it for her, and for the child, and how that made it so there was a part of him that hated her and hated the child too. He could tell her how he had to change something, and this was the only thing that had any give.

He thought maybe it would do good to mention how he still loved her. She had something very special in her that still got to him down deep, when he thought about it. And then he'd finish off by telling her about Angie. He wouldn't get into how things would be different with Angie. He wouldn't get into how things were going to change when he left. Not now. Not in this letter. He'd just write the things he knew so far, leave it for her to find, and be done with it.

He looked around the kitchen and considered how to start the letter. Should he include the word *dear* or not? He didn't know in this case. Stale cupcakes on the counter caught his eye, and a thought came into his mind from far back. He was thinking of how she'd baked a small cake just for their son for his first birthday party. The boy scooped it up with his hands and rubbed it all over his face, while everyone laughed. He thought of the way her face looked then, when she was very young.

> *Honey,*
> *I have decided to leave. When it comes right down to it, I cannot*
> *tell you why. I am leaving you for no reason. I have the things*
> *that are mine. Everything that's left is yours.*
> *I'm sorry.*
> *Matthew*

He folded the letter and put it in an envelope. He scribbled *To My Wife* on the front. He stood up and looked around the room. He was thinking, now, of places where he could put it. He thought it was important for her to find it right away. He wanted to find somewhere she'd see it as soon as she walked through the door, because he didn't like the thought of her calling out to him, thinking he was home, in the other room, and then finding it.

He considered taping it to the door. But it would alarm her if she saw it there; she'd think it had something to do with their son. The coffee table might work. He could put it there. But then again there was a chance she might not see it right away. She might not see it until after she had already settled in. She'd have her shoes off, and maybe even her sweatpants on, and she'd be sipping her Coke by the time it caught her eye. She'd read the letter and she'd fall over on the couch, head in her knees like when her father died. She might stay all night like that. It was too much. It'd catch her off guard if he left it on the coffee table. No. It was important for her to get it before the feelings of home got inside.

He thought about leaving it right there on the kitchen table. She'd hang the car keys on the hook, and then she'd see it. But he used to leave love letters there for her to find, way back when they were working opposite shifts. It gave her something to come home to. She'd see it and she'd think of those old letters. She'd feel something inside. He could hear her saying, "Matthew, you didn't have to do that," as she picked it up.

THE SHORT HISTORY OF HER HEART

Pain from panic attacks. Heart attack. Angioplasty. A stent put in. A second angioplasty. Calcified. Crystallized. Shattered. Another heart attack. She was rushed by ambulance to the city, where they took it out, cleaned it out, stripped an artery from her leg and sewed it in.

Her father died. My father left her. Her mother died. And we all grew up and moved away.

For the irregular heartbeats, they electrocuted her. When that didn't work they implanted a pacemaker. She feels it at night. Shocking her back to life.

The Songs We Used to Sing

A year after my mother died, I went back east to her house in Upstate New York to sort through her belongings. My mother had moved in with my sister in her last years, and she'd rented our old house out to one of the many Bosnian families who had immigrated to the area after the war. They were still living there now. It was a small house on Culver Avenue, which sat on a quiet block with two other houses between a barbershop and a florist. My sister was planning to sell it later that year. I wanted to look through our old things in the attic before someone came and cleaned everything out.

My sister had already been by and had taken what she wanted. When I got to the house a man and a woman greeted me at the front door. I was surprised that they had not removed my mother's TRUST IN THE LORD sign from the small square of glass above the peephole. This was the first time I'd been back since her funeral. It was a frigid day in March just as it had been on the day of my last visit. My husband and daughter were with me on that occasion, but now we all agreed it would be easier if I made the trip alone.

"You must be Enis," I said to the man when he opened the door. He was a cheery man with dark hair and a large, square face. "I'm Teresa's daughter," I said. "Valerie."

"Yes," he said. "Come in, come in," he said, opening the door and making a space for me in the narrow hallway. A gust of piercing-cold wind blew in behind me. His light brown eyes sparkled when he smiled. He was dressed in a thick wool sweater that looked to be hand-knitted. I had the strange sensation that I'd known him for a long time. His wife wore a simple dress and no makeup. Her blond hair was pulled into a braid that was tied at the end with a ribbon. Her face was pretty, with sharp features: high cheekbones, an elegant nose, and a prominent chin. "This is my wife," he said, "Irma." Her handshake was delicate and her eyes stayed down.

To get to the attic we had to go through the house. The smell of roasting meat and onions drifted through all the rooms. It was surprising to smell other people's food in our old home. My mother used to make tomato sauce and meatballs on Sundays, and that was how I remembered it smelling. She had rented it out furnished and everything else was the same.

"Everything looks great," I said. It did. My mother was not much of a housekeeper and I rarely saw the place looking so clean. The wood coffee table was polished and the carpet still had lines from the vacuum. Then, "I'll just be upstairs," I said. "I promise not to get in your way."

A young girl darted out from behind the rocking chair and went behind another chair on the other side of the room. She peeked her face out from behind the second chair, then looked up at her mother. "Tell her I'm four," she whispered loudly. Her dark hair was cut into a bob with curved bangs in the middle of her forehead. I wondered if she had cut the bangs herself.

Irma scooped her up and smiled. "This is Miranda," she said. "She's four."

The girl buried her face in her mother's neck and kicked her feet gently. She had her mother's nose and strong chin, but Enis's kind eyes.

"Wow," I said to her. "That's big." When her eyes peeked out again I said, "Is this your bedroom?" When she nodded I said, "That used to be my room too."

I looked in. The queen-sized bed was in the corner where it had been when Dana and I shared the room twenty years ago. A small aquarium on her dresser shot flickers of pink light around the room, illuminating several of her paintings that hung on the wall.

"I like your pictures," I said.

"I have a fish," she said, opening her eyes wide and twirling a piece of hair from the side of her head. "Her name is Ariel."

"Will Dana be coming today?" Enis said.

"That's a pretty name for a fish," I said. Then I turned to Enis. "No," I said, "just me today."

"If you need help, I—"

"That's okay," I said, "I'm mostly just going to be going through things today, that's all. No heavy lifting," I said.

"We love this place," Irma said, looking suddenly sad. "There's good energy here. We've been very happy here." She looked around.

"Your mother was a wonderful woman," Enis said then. "She was always very kind to us," he said. "We're very sorry for your loss."

When he said this I thought of my mother in the kitchen long ago, washing the dishes. Orange suds from her tomato sauce ran up her arms halfway to her elbows. When I walked past her she looked up at me and smiled. She was singing one of the songs we used to sing. *"There's milk and honey in that land. There's milk and honey in that land. There's milk and honey in that land, where I'm bound."*

Thinking of it I felt nothing. "Thank you," I said to Enis. "She was." I lowered my eyes and made my way up the dark staircase to the attic.

I didn't cry at my mother's funeral and I hadn't felt much in the year that followed. Once in a while I'd dream of her and I'd wake up with tears in my eyes. That was as close as I came to feeling. Time had become fuzzy and the entire year had passed more or less without me. It was as if I were floating above myself, watching my life unfold, but I wasn't quite the one living it. Something had severed within me. I didn't know if it would heal back again.

Once, when my daughter was still a baby, I brought her into the bathroom with me so I could take a shower. She was sitting happily in her bouncy seat, kicking her legs and making cooing sounds. I got into the shower and when I shut the thick glass door behind me, I heard a loud creaking sound. The hinge had broken and the door was jammed shut. I slammed into the door, but it wouldn't budge. I slammed it again and again. Nothing. After a while, my daughter started to cry. I knew my husband wouldn't be home for several hours. I tried and tried, but I couldn't make the door budge. I pulled at the handle so hard I felt the ligaments in my shoulder rip from the bone. I couldn't shatter the glass either, it was way too thick. Eventually I sat on the shower floor. I knew that I hadn't escaped grief, that it was waiting for me, and that one day it would find me, but it was like this now with my feelings. I could see them. They were screaming out to me. But there was nothing, and I mean nothing, I could do to get to them.

My family took comfort in religion. They believed that my mother was in a better place now, that she had been made young again, made new. At the funeral my aunt came to me, with what seemed to be genuine gladness, and said, "No more knee pain. No more bad heart. She's dancing in heaven now."

The pastor went on and on about it too, the wonderful life she was living now, and all the dear old friends she was surely reuniting with in heaven as we sat there in a pale blue room staring at her dead body in an ivory casket. She looked pretty, though not at all like herself. For one thing, she never wore makeup, and she had a lot of it on now. My sister had picked out a burgundy dress for her to wear, though her favorite color had always been pink. This bothered me immensely. But I was happy to know that inside the coffin, she was wearing the slippers I'd bought her for Christmas. They were good slippers, made of lamb's wool, with an inch of soft shearling inside; she'd loved them, and it comforted me to know that her feet would be warm.

The pastor told us to imagine it, that right then, she might be meeting God. A palpable excitement flooded the funeral parlor when he said this, as if we were all sitting at the same table with the winner of a rare and exceptional award whose name had just been called. All my life I had believed in God. Right up through the time of her last illness I prayed every day. But it was this, their certainty that she was in heaven, and the comfort they took from it, that made me sure none of it was real.

The smell of the meat and the onions made its way into the attic too. It made my mouth water and my stomach growl. It was cold up there and I kept my coat on. The attic was much like it had been all those years ago: all of our stuff piled up just past the stairs. Heaps and heaps of closed boxes. Beyond the boxes was a little area set up like a living room, with a torn loveseat, two antique chairs, a carpet, and a small wooden coffee table that was cracked in the middle. A glass lamp with no shade sat on the floor beside the loveseat, and on the coffee table were a few very old magazines. My brother liked to sit up there as a teenager, smoke his cigarettes, and practice playing his guitar. We'd hear his music throughout the house. Past the little living room area was some more broken furniture scattered about and a few hanging dress bags. A beam of light shone through the window, making the dust sparkle like glitter. Everything was covered in a layer of dirt and cobwebs. I worried about spiders, rats.

I sat down in the center of the boxes and started opening them. The task was daunting. There was so much to sort through, and I'd lived without it all of my adult life. Now that I was there I didn't know what the point was. I considered leaving. I started opening the boxes. Mostly they were filled with everyone's old clothes. Winter clothes. Summer clothes. I peeked inside but nothing looked familiar, except a red-and-white Snoopy sweatshirt that I'd loved as a child. I put it in the box of things that I would keep. Other boxes were filled with various art things: pictures we drew, none of them signed, so there was no way of knowing which one of us had made them; crayons; dried-up paints, and stiffened paintbrushes. There were boxes of old notebooks and textbooks from high school and college. Boxes of stuffed animals and dolls. Boxes of bedding. Boxes of lace curtains. Boxes of Christmas decorations. Then boxes of my mother's: her clothes, her kitchen supplies, her old photographs, her trinkets.

A few hours after I started looking through everything, I heard the stairs creaking and saw Enis's warm smile. He was carrying a tall glass of water. The ice clanked against the glass as he walked over to me. He handed the water to me and sat down on one of the boxes a few feet away from where I was sitting. "So what is it you're looking for, anyway?" he said gently.

"I don't know," I said, feeling discouraged. I drank most of the water. "Things that were mine, I guess."

There was a cowboy hat on the floor and he picked it up, and dusted it off, and put it on his head. He smiled. "Was this yours?" he said.

"No," I said, laughing. "That was my brother's."

From a box of toys he picked up an action figure that had frizzy black hair. It was dressed in a sleeveless black leotard, cut low, so that most of its muscled chest was exposed. Its face was painted white with a black star over the right eye. The lips were red. Enis held it out, looking confused, then lowered his eyebrows and looked at me.

"Don't look at me," I said, shaking my head. "That was Dana's."

He studied it for a moment longer, then shrugged and tossed it back. There was something playful in the way he did it, and it made me laugh. He walked around, peeking into the boxes. I didn't mind him looking at our things and was glad for the company. I realized that he reminded me of my high school Spanish teacher, Mr. Castillo: a boisterous man with bushy gray eyebrows who once stood on his desk and belted out a song from *West Side Story*. Enis put his hand into a box of stuffed animals and felt around. After a minute he held up a floppy stuffed lamb. "What's this?" he asked. "Was this yours?"

"It was," I said, smiling. "I took it everywhere with me when I was a kid and slept with it at night," I said. I hadn't thought of it in years and felt touched to see it. He handed it over to me, and out of instinct I gave it a squeeze. Then I remembered that the sound box had broken. "See this," I said to Enis, pointing at what looked like a scar up the length of the lamb's stomach. "It used to talk," I said. "When the voice box broke, my mom did a surgery on it and filled it with something soft."

Enis's eyes sparkled. "That's sweet," he said. "You should take that," he said.

I put the lamb in the box of things that I was taking. "She liked to sew," I said. "She was always making little clothes for our dolls."

He walked through the boxes, every once in a while grabbing something, looking at it quickly, then putting it back. "We never get up here," he said. "Well, that's not exactly true. My daughter, the young one, you met her, Miranda, she likes to hide up here sometimes." He walked over toward the dirty window. You could see some light through it but that was all. It was too dirty to see the world below: the little yard with the pussy willow tree, the garage, and beyond that the alley that led to Humbert Avenue. A loose board on the floor squeaked and settled as he came back over. "Some mornings we're looking for her, and we can't find her, and then we remember that she might be up here."

After a minute, flipping through the pages of a sketchbook, he asked, "Who was the artist?"

"That was my mother," I said, reaching for it. I thought of the angels she was always drawing when I was young. She'd framed one, and it hung in our living room for most of my childhood. My sister had it now, hanging in her own living room. We used a scan of it on her prayer card at the funeral. I remembered sitting at the kitchen table and watching her draw, how magically something lifelike would emerge when she put a pencil to the paper.

The last time I saw her was not long before she died. She had been hospitalized for an infection in her foot, and after that she had to go to a rehabilitation center so she could get back to caring for herself in the most fundamental of ways. This meant standing up and walking fifteen feet to the bathroom with her walker, sitting down, standing back up again, and getting herself back to her bed. My husband, my young daughter, and I flew in from California for the week to help keep her spirits up.

On the last morning of our visit, there was an outbreak of the flu in her wing of the rehabilitation center. My daughter was not allowed inside. I went alone and had breakfast with her in the cafeteria. It was nearly empty aside from a very old man who was a patient there, and his wife, a visitor, who kept asking the nurse to please bring her husband his morning coffee. My mother looked off ahead, staring blankly at a large painting on the wall in front of her. Her short hair had grown out white except for a few inches of black still at the tips. She'd always been a big woman, tall and heavy, but now she seemed withered and frail in her wheelchair. The painting was of a winter scene at night: a small cottage with glowing windows amid fields of glittering snow. "I like that painting," she said, finally. "Look at the light."

I knew this could be the last time I saw her. A sea of emotion swelled inside me. There was a thickness in my throat and I felt certain I would break down crying if I tried to talk. I often felt this way when it was time to say goodbye to my mother. She had never been in good health, and from the time I was a child I worried she could die at any moment. She had, in fact, escaped death many times. Surviving two heart attacks, a bypass surgery, a septic infection, and even a stroke. I looked out at the painting. On the branch of one of the trees sat a red bird. "It looks like a Thomas Kinkade," I said.

"I don't know," she said, staring out.

We were both quiet, still looking at the painting. A few minutes later, "It seems like just yesterday," she started to say, then paused for what felt like a very long time. I thought she might start in with a memory of my childhood. I'd always stayed close to her when I was young. If someone were to have asked me who my best friend was, through the time I was in my twenties, I would have said her name. We had been very close. But after I moved away, a distance settled between us that I could never quite penetrate, as much as I would have liked to. She went on. "It seems like just yesterday you were home," she said. "You'd shut yourself in your room. You were always shutting yourself in your room."

I caught my breath. "When?" I said. "When I was in high school?"

"No," she said. "When you'd come home from college. I'd be so excited to see you, then you'd shut yourself in your room."

"Yes," I said, though this was not how I remembered it.

"You went there and you screwed it up," she said. "You had that scholarship and you lost it."

"Yes," I said. "I messed everything up."

"You lost that computer too. Then you had to have that procedure."

"Yes," I said. "I was so irresponsible. I lost the computer. It was my fault. I left it where it could be stolen."

"You did. You were," she said. "And you had to have that procedure."

The nurse came over with her pills. My mother dumped them onto her tray where they mixed with the syrup from her pancakes. She placed them on her tongue, one by one, grunting and closing her eyes as if the pills were slicing her throat as she swallowed them.

When she was done she stared blankly out at the painting again. After a few minutes I wheeled her back to her room without saying anything. I put her where she liked to sit, where she could best see the TV. A rerun of *The Golden Girls* was playing, and she started to watch it. I put the rolling table in front of her, gave her her crossword puzzle book, her pen, and her reading glasses. I filled her cup of ice water. "Goodbye, Mom," I said.

She didn't look up at me; she was watching the TV, half smiling at something Blanche was saying. "Goodbye," she said, still laughing a little at the show.

I bent down and hugged her then, let my head linger for a while on her chest. She'd always worn perfume that smelled like cinnamon. I thought I almost smelled it now, though I knew it had probably been years since she'd put it on. I heard her heart beating. I was unable to hold back my tears anymore.

She looked up at me, reached her hand out, and blessed my forehead with the sign of the cross. She'd done it every night before I went to bed, and before every time I left the house, too. "Thank you for this locket," she said. I'd brought her a locket with a picture of both of us in it. *So we'll always be together,* I'd told her. She wore it the whole time I was there. "I must have done something right," she said, "to raise a daughter so thoughtful. That's something."

"I love you, Mom," I said, and I left, and a week later she died, and that was the last time I saw her.

In the attic, Enis picked up my brother's old guitar and sat on the loveseat. "Was this yours?" he said.

"It was my brother's," I said.

He held it at a distance, examined it for a minute, then started to tune it.

"Do you play?" I asked him.

"A little," he said. "Here and there," he said. "I used to."

He set the guitar back where it was and sat next to me and smiled. "Tell me," he said. "What's it like being back?" he said. "I often wonder what it would be like to be back after all this time." He looked off, sliding the backs of his fingernails over his lips several times. "Sometimes I dream I'm back there," he said. "Everyone thinks of the war. But Bosnia is actually a very beautiful place." He stared off. "The rivers and the mountains," he said. "It's not like anywhere else. You've never seen anything so beautiful."

I was surprised to hear him speak of it so fondly. My images of Bosnia were images of devastation and ash that came from the news around the time I was in high school. That was when all the refugees flooded into Utica, filling the homes that had been left vacant when everyone's kids from my generation moved away for better jobs. People rejected the Bosnians at first, felt they were taking over, but that changed later when it became clear that they'd saved the city, rebuilding the broken-down houses and reopening the closed stores and restaurants.

"Being back?" I said after a while. "It makes me feel old," I said. "It makes me feel like the road has been very long," I said. It did. My life there in that house felt as far away as the stars. He looked at me and I could see that he wanted to hear more. I went on. "When I lived here," I said. "I'd go to school every day. We'd go to church on Sundays. We'd play in the yard," I said. "On the weekends we'd go to my aunt's house, or else my cousins would come over," I said. "I thought that was life."

He nodded and I could see that he understood what I meant. "I was in the house with my mother and father," he said, "and I heard the grenades. Everything happened very fast after that, and then we were gone." He looked off. "I didn't know it would be the last time we'd share that space together." After a moment he stood up, looked in the boxes again. He pulled a rusty tin church out from one of the boxes, wound the top, and it played "Amazing Grace." He offered it to me, and I put it in the box of things that I would keep. It was something my mother had loved. "But I can't complain," he went on after a minute. "I've been here for twenty-two years," he said. "I've married the love of my life."

He went back to the loveseat, picked up the guitar again, and started to play something that sounded familiar. Then he started to sing something in Bosnian. His voice was deep and pure and I watched as the song overtook him. He lifted his face and closed his eyes as he sang. I didn't know what he was singing, but I could see that whatever the words meant, they were very true to him, and it struck something in me to see this. I sat quietly, just listening. I felt my breath slow and the tiny muscles throughout my body settle. I closed my eyes.

"What's going on up there," I heard Irma say after a few minutes. She was coming up the stairs. "We heard music," she said. Miranda ran ahead of her and started grabbing things from the boxes. Her hair was wet now, brushed back, and she was wearing a nightgown under her hoodie. She grabbed a Barbie doll from one of the boxes and started to braid its hair. "Can I own this," she said, looking at me.

"Of course," I said.

Irma set a plate of some kind of pastry on the small coffee table. She gestured toward it, and I stood and took a slice immediately. It was flaky, covered with melted cream cheese, and sprinkled with confectionary sugar. It was delicious, still warm from the oven, sweet and savory at once.

Enis was still singing softly. "Look at him," Irma said. "Always with the sad music," she said. "Why don't you play something happy for a change?"

Enis stood up when she said this, as if awakening from a trance. He looked to his right and then to his left. "You want happy?" he said. He started to clap his hands. "The lady asks for happy," he said. "Okay, we've got happy here," he said. "We can do happy here." He began singing some kind of folk song in Bosnian. He kicked out one leg, then the other, and put his hands on his waist and twisted his hips in an exaggerated way.

Irma's face turned pink, then red, and she covered it with both of her hands. "No," she said, laughing. "Not that," she said. "Don't," she said. "Please, don't."

This only fueled Enis, who closed his eyes and put his face up and continued hopping around in a circle. He sang the song louder and louder, repeating the chorus over and over again every minute or so. Miranda started laughing and stood in front of him. She lifted the skirt of her nightgown and twirled around. Enis took her hand and they spun and twirled together. They kicked up their legs in unison. Irma was laughing too. She looked at me, her face still red, took my hand for a moment, squeezed it, patted it, then let it go and joined in the dancing. They all linked arms and moved together in a circle, lifting their legs at the same time. I sat there watching, listening to Enis sing, to the sound of their laughter. Miranda's eyes sparkled just like his as she laughed. I could feel her innocence, her love. It occurred to me that she might remember this moment. She might think of it one day when she is older, long after Enis and Irma are gone, and she lives somewhere else, maybe somewhere far away, with other people who are strangers to her now, if they have even been born at all yet. She might tell someone about the woman who came to look in the attic, how she didn't take much, just a small box of things that she could carry by herself, and how as she sat there watching them dance, she started to cry.

Maybe there was a name for the dance they were doing. She might say that name, and the person she's talking to might know exactly what it looked like, might understand just how happy they must have been there, in that moment.

In Moments of Silence

All morning the baby was crying. And this was after a long night: five wakings to nurse. It was easier now that the baby was in the bed with her, but the mother was exhausted. It had been seven months and there was no one to help her. It surprised her how hard it really was to care for a baby. The thing was, there were no breaks. She loved the baby. Adored her. The baby looked just like her. She was thankful for this. The same blue eyes and dark hair. The baby was an absolute joy, a true pleasure. But the mother was so tired. When she was younger she'd fantasized about things, usually illicit sex with older men or younger women. Now what she fantasized about—and really found herself yearning for in almost the same aching way—was going to a hotel room alone, closing the curtains, and sleeping for twenty-four hours straight.

One Tuesday afternoon she put the baby down in the crib and the baby started to cry. It was the hearty, red-faced, mouth-wide-open, breath-holding-until-she-turns-blue cry. The mother hated this cry. This cry hurt the mother, physically made her breasts ache and leak. But the mother had to pee. Was it too much to ask that the baby give her one goddamn minute to pee? "I'll be right back, Baby," she called out. "I'm coming, Baby," she called out again, this time louder. The mother worried about how clingy the baby had become but remembered hearing that a strong attachment now actually meant the baby would be more independent later. So she did what she could to foster the attachment: she wore the baby in a sling, shared her bed, and nursed her whenever the baby wanted. It was intense, nonstop mothering. Sometimes her head would spin at how fast a day, a week, went in this way, with this work.

But in the bathroom the screams were relentless, disturbing. "Give Mama a minute," she called out again, an edge in her voice. But the baby kept right on crying. The mother wondered about her choices. Maybe she should have taken the doctor's advice when the baby was very young and just let her cry it out. But the mother wondered what must the baby go through all those hours alone in the dark. Wouldn't it change something in the baby, make a dent? Then, at once, she noticed the baby had stopped crying entirely. Her first impulse was to run to her, but she knew that in moments of silence, you're not supposed to go. Silence means they're learning to self-soothe. Don't interrupt her, they said. So she decided to take a shower.

When she was finished she heard the faint murmur of language from the room. Her heart dropped with the familiar fear that a stranger had entered her home. She held her breath and hurried to the room. "Baby!" she cried out when she looked into the crib. "Where's my baby!" she screamed. Inside the crib was a young woman. "What have you done with my baby," the mother cried.

"Very funny, Mama," the young woman said. The woman looked just like her.

The mother felt like she was going to pass out. She had issues with her blood pressure and felt it must be getting low now. A wave of nausea warmed her head, then rolled down through her shoulders and into her chest. She felt chills in her jaw.

"Where is she?" the mother said.

"Mama," the young woman said. "What are you talking about?" she said. She had the mother's high cheekbones, her curly dark hair, and for a second fear gave way to pride: her daughter was beautiful.

The mother did not know if she was awake or dreaming. There was a swirling feeling in her head and she thought she might vomit. Her knees tickled, and her ankles were weak. "You're not my baby," she said. "You must be twenty years old."

The young woman stood and stretched her long leg over the side of the crib. "You're losing it, Mama," she said. Then, "Did you take your medicine today?" she said. There was an icy tone in her voice that the mother identified right away as meanness. The young woman moved from the crib to the bathroom, where she took a red lipstick from the drawer and rubbed it over her lips. "I'm going out with Joel tonight," she said. "I'll be home in the morning."

The mother gasped. No, this wasn't right. No. Something had gone horribly wrong. She'd had the sense that all time was folding in on her and she couldn't see which moments were old, which were new. But she knew what to do. She knew the way to care for her daughter. Knew how to calm her. She pulled the young woman close. Tiny droplets of milk formed on the holes in her nipple as she felt the pressure under her arms release. She tickled the young woman under her chin, but the woman would not latch. The mother tried again, this time making an areola sandwich the way the lactation consultant had shown her. Still nothing. The mother tried to lift the young woman, to bring her closer so they'd be skin to skin; she could rock her, or else walk her around the room. But the young woman wiggled and squirmed until she was free. Then the mother had an idea. She sang "Twinkle, Twinkle, Little Star," replacing the words halfway through the way she did it every night, singing instead, "Mama loves the baby girl. Mama loves the baby girl," over and over. But even this, her nighttime song, had no effect. It was all the mother knew to try. These were her things. None of them worked. Nothing worked. There was no way for her to still the baby. Her only choice was to let her go.

On the Other Side of the Yard

Early one September morning, the summer my husband and I moved from New York to Los Angeles, we saw a couple we almost knew lose their son at a park about a mile from our house. We saw him climb a high tree. We saw him fall to the ground. We saw everyone circle around.

By the time we got over there a woman was performing CPR. Someone else had called for an ambulance.

"Keep trying," the mother, whose name we remembered was Brittany, said. She was lying on the ground next to the boy. She was not crying. We understood this meant she was in shock.

Her husband stood back, watching. He was the one who had been standing under the tree smiling up at the boy when he fell.

All morning my husband had been annoyed with me. We were there with our two-year-old daughter. There was a baby squirrel running around the park making a screaming sound. It ran up one man's leg, then back down again.

"It needs help," I said. "It's going to hurt someone. A kid."

The older kids were chasing it around, laughing each time it screamed.

"This is too stressful," my husband said. "Can't you just relax," he said. "It'll run away," he said, spotting our daughter as she climbed up the slide. "It's just a squirrel. Leave it alone."

I tried to relax, but the screaming.

"I'm going to call someone," I said after a while. My husband rolled his eyes. It was true, I did lean a bit too heavily on the police. I called for suspicious cars parked on our street, noises in the night, neighbors having heated disputes in the middle of the afternoon.

They put me through to the Department of Animal Services, who said there was nothing they could do for an uninjured wild animal.

I went back to my husband who received this news as smugly as I thought he would. He'd been pushing our daughter on the swing for thirty minutes. If you've ever done it, then you know: there is nothing in the world more boring than pushing a child on a swing for thirty minutes. I was thankful that it was the weekend, that it was my husband's arms, not mine, doing the pushing.

"Don't look now," my husband said, prompting me to immediately turn my head and look.

He went on with a sigh. "Isn't that the family who came to our house?" he said. "For the table?"

I looked again, this time as if to take in the park: the large weeping willow trees; a mother yelling at her kid on the play structure; a baby getting his diaper changed in the grassy area; and, oh, thank God, someone else cared—a young father luring the baby squirrel out of a tree with some nuts and a bucket. Then, yes, there was the family who came to our house a month before. Their son was fast on the stairs. At the top of the slide he held the bar and swung.

We were selling an old dining room table that we'd brought with us from New York. Turned legs, pine. It had belonged to my first husband's grandmother. After he died I held on to it out of loyalty, but now I'd read a book on letting things go. *Hold it in your hands,* the book had suggested of everything, *and ask yourself if it brings you joy.* It was an easy enough question, but a hard thing to know. What in your life really brought you joy? The woman responded to the ad we posted on Craigslist within minutes. My husband arranged a time for them to come, and on Saturday morning promptly at nine o'clock they pulled up in front of our house in an old pickup truck.

The woman was about twenty-five with wild hair. She got out of the truck, then released a young boy, who had the same wild hair, from the back.

I was reluctant about letting people into our home. I'd read the statistics on burglaries, how most of the time it was someone you knew: a maid, a gardener, a neighbor. But in the emails the woman was polite. She signed off "take good care," which felt somehow like the voice of an old friend.

Behind her, a young man dragged his feet as he walked. He wore big sneakers, baggy jeans. His dark hair was covered by a baseball cap that he had tipped sideways. The hat read—was it? Yes. *What an bitches?*

"Come on in," I said, smiling. The woman looked back at the young man. Her face was pretty. Green eyes, freckles. "This is Jack," she said, "I'm Brittany." She scooped up her son and walked into the house.

My husband came from over on the other side of the room. "It's just back here," he said, "in the yard. We have it outside but it's covered. There hasn't been rain in a while, so."

Brittany walked with my husband. Jack and I followed behind. Our daughter showed him her wooden puppy. When she pulled the string to walk it, its ears flapped and its tail wagged. "Puppy," she said to Jack.

He got down to her level and smiled. "Is this your puppy?" he said. "Is this your little doggy?" He took the string and pulled the dog along. My daughter was delighted. She buried her face in my leg and laughed.

"You look familiar," I heard Brittany say to my husband. This happened a lot since he was on *Lost*. Most people recognized him but no one could ever quite place him. He was always cast as the weirdo in everything he did. The mad scientist. The cult leader. Or, for an indie he was filming now, he played the teacher who was suspected of taking the kid. For this role he had to grow his hair long. On weekends he wore it in a low ponytail.

"You do too," I heard my husband say. Then, "Here she is. A beauty," he said. "Solid pine." It was silent for a moment. Then, "Belonged to my grandmother," he added.

I caught his eye, surprised to hear this false history.

The three of them walked around the table, sliding their fingers over the top.

"Look at those turned legs," my husband said. "They don't make them like this anymore."

Brittany bent and looked at the underside of the table. "We've been looking for one like this," she said. She examined the joinery, the screws. She gave it a shake, then ran her hand over the surface again. "A little rough," she said.

"Rustic," my husband said.

She looked at Jack. "What do you think, babe?" she said.

"Up to you," Jack said, taking in the yard. He looked at my husband and said, "I don't get involved."

My husband smiled. "I hear you, buddy," he said.

After a minute Brittany said to Jack, "It'll be your table, too," she said. She went to him and pulled him by the arm. "Come on," she said. "Sit down. Let's see if it fits."

My husband rested his hand on my back. "Let us get out of your way," he said to Brittany. "Take as long as you want."

He was the only man who'd come anywhere near me after September 11. He was not afraid of it, my pain. What I didn't know before was that people avoid people who have been through a trauma as if it's contagious. It was not contagious. If you talked to me, your husband was not going to be blown to pieces in a falling tower. For a while there was a certain comfort in the collective grieving of the entire world. But then the entire world moved on.

Through the window in the kitchen we could see them at the table.

Jack sat down at one end. Brittany at the other. Their son had found the trampoline and was jumping over on the other side of the yard.

We watched them. Brittany smiled at Jack, blushing. It seemed they were brand-new to each other, like she was still nervous around him, still trying to win him in some essential way he'd not yet been won. She tapped her long nails on the tabletop, laughed each time he spoke. Their lips were moving. We couldn't make out what they were saying, but anyone could see that it was flirtation.

I looked at my husband. He looked at me. We both looked away.

A few minutes later they were all inside again. "We love it," Brittany said. "Would you take six hundred?"

I felt something inside of me shift, a coolness spill into my jaw. "Oh," I said. "I don't know," I said. "We mentioned in the ad that the price was firm."

It was quiet for a moment. No one said anything. Then I added, "A thousand dollars is fair for this table. If anything, it's low," I said.

"We don't have a thousand," Jack said. "But we have six hundred in cash right here," he said, flashing money from his wallet. He looked at my husband and lifted his eyebrows. "If you can help me get it into my truck," he said, "we can take it off your hands right now."

"I'm sorry," I said, shaking my head. "This belonged to my husband's grandmother." I pictured him then, my first husband, at his spot on the side of the table. He liked to sit there on weekend mornings and eat sugary cereal from a giant coffee mug.

My husband lowered his eyes. I saw a terrible sadness fall over Brittany's face. She moved closer to Jack. "That's okay," she said in a soft voice. "We understand," she said. She scooped up her son and they made their way through the house and out the front door.

My husband sat on the couch and stared at the television. I sat beside him without saying anything. "You could have just given it to them," he said finally. "It's four hundred dollars," he said. "Who cares."

"People think they can take whatever they want," I said. "You can't just give it to them."

Now, a month later, we stood near the tree with everyone else watching. My husband took our daughter for a walk to get her away from what was happening. By the time the ambulance arrived, the boy's curly hair was covered in blood. He had not moved. The EMTs tried to resuscitate him, then gave up. When they stopped, Brittany's face turned red, purple. She ran to Jack and started slapping at him. She screamed. She punched at his chest with the balls of her hands. She dug her long nails into his cheeks and scratched down. "What did you do?" she screamed. "What did you do?" Jack stood still and let her beat him. After a moment, an EMT pulled her away, covered her shoulders with a blanket, sat her down in the shade of a willow tree. As this was happening two other men moved the boy onto a stretcher.

Brittany did not move. She sat there, still. Her eyes were closed, her body rocking. I wondered if she was meditating, saying a prayer. I knew that a part of her was escaping, forever leaving this broken place.

I went to her, touched her shoulder. She looked up at me, her green eyes scanning, confused, frightened. "I know you," I said.

IF THERE'S ANYTHING YOU NEED

Laura's sixteen-year-old nephew, Mike, was visiting from Frank-
fort, New York. He was traveling as an unaccompanied minor.
Laura had arranged the ticket. For an additional seventy-five dollars
each way, an airline representative would escort him through security
and to his gate, supervise him during the flight, then lead him to the
baggage claim department where Laura's husband, William, would
meet him. Laura was glad William had agreed to pick him up. The
Los Angeles freeways were a thing she never could get used to, even
after nearly a decade of living in the city. Cars ripping by you at eighty
miles an hour. And those exits! Get in the wrong lane and before
you know it you're on another highway heading for the desert. Did
that once. Halfway to Palm Springs before she figured out how to
right herself.

She was nervous about seeing him. There was a closeness between
them, sure, that was true, but she feared it might be awkward with no
other family there to split the conversation. They'd kept in touch, with
emails and phone calls, but she hadn't been back east in a while. The
last time, she recalled, was just after she and William had eloped about

three years ago. She worried about the boy. Lately she had a sense he was on the wrong path.

Mike stumbled in ahead of William, his face in his cell phone, his thumbs working the tiny silver buttons. He took big, heavy steps, not paying much attention to where he was going. Seeing him, Laura felt a flash of fear, as if a stranger were making his way through her home. He was tall now, and thick and muscular-looking. And there was something else: *holes* in both of his earlobes the size of pennies. They were framed by metal earrings that looked like bolts. His dark hair hit his shoulders in soft waves. He gathered it with his hand and held it away from his face.

"Aunt Laura," he said, smiling, his eyes the shape of half-moons. He slipped his phone into his pocket and came at her, slightly lifting her as he hugged her.

Had he shot up. Six feet now. It made her feel like crying when she saw him.

He looked more like his mother too. There came the flood of sadness and regret when she thought of her sister Shannon. Since Shannon and her drinking had gone from something casual to something serious, there wasn't room in her life for anything else. Could not keep a job or apartment. A steady stream of casual boyfriends moving in, moving out. She had a habit of always disappearing. When Mike was younger, she'd leave him in the care of neighbors for days on end. More recently she'd leave him home alone. Laura did what she could to help: encouraged rehab, encouraged AA, sent money for Mike's school clothes. But in the same way you can't talk to someone who's drunk when you're sober, eventually, she let go of her sister.

"Mikey," she said, rubbing his arm.

"Mike," he said.

Then, as if he noticed her reaction to his ears, he wiggled his little finger through one of the holes at her. Told her they were *gauged*.

Said that it was something everyone was doing now. Laura set a piece of her brown hair behind her ear and told him it looked cool. She didn't want him to see how it affected her. Inside she was thinking: an outward expression of what's inside. She was thinking: *maimed*.

But he was clearly still at ease around her, and this made her feel good. "This place is awesome," he said, drawing out the first sylla-ble. As he looked around, Laura became self-conscious. Since marrying William she'd taken to certain luxuries. Their house was tiny for Santa Monica, but it was sunny and new. Not at all like the old one-bedroom apartment in the valley she'd rented for all those years. Hard to believe how far a nurse's salary *didn't* get you in Los Angeles.

Now their home was decorated in the bare style that William, a neurologist, favored: white sofas with tufted cushions and delicate legs, a round shag rug on the hardwood floor, and carefully placed art on the walls. They had central air, and it was set right, but Laura always felt cold. She checked it now.

"Is that HD?" the boy said. His eyes were wide on the flat-screen television that covered a good part of one living room wall. He had a habit of twirling a piece of hair from the top of his head after every-thing he said. And there was a nervous blink Laura noticed; this was new. The stale scent of patchouli and cigarettes from his clothes made her nose sting.

"Just got it a few months ago." William was sitting on the couch already. He had the television going with a rerun, but the volume was turned off. For a moment, they all rested their eyes on the silent woman's talking face.

"No traffic then?" Laura asked.

"Not a bit," said William. He was a tall man with thinning gray hair and a foxy face.

"And they brought him right to baggage?" she asked. "Did they give you any problems?"

"No. Just showed the woman my ID, and she handed him right over."

William stood up and left the room. A few minutes later he was back with three icy Cokes and a plate of chocolate-chip cookies that Laura had baked especially for her nephew. They all sat down around the glass coffee table.

"How are things at the restaurant?" Laura asked Mike. He'd told her the news about his quitting high school in an email. Last month Shannon drove him to the school and waited in her car while he signed the papers to quit. It flattened Laura when she heard it. She pictured the boy signing his name. Signing on for a life of making ends meet, making the rent, making himself get out of bed in the morning.

Unlike his mother, she'd been talking to him about the importance of a good education from the time he was very young. Last year, she'd even contacted some schools, had brochures sent, hoping to pique some latent interest. He liked to draw, why not a career in art? And there was always financial aid, scholarships. She'd managed, so could he. But, as her mother used to say, some things were like spitting into the ocean. So maybe this had been one. He'd taken a job as a busboy at the restaurant where his mother waited tables. Laura let herself have a breath before shifting her glance in his direction. She smiled warmly, hoping tenderness came through, not sorrow.

"I know you wanted me to go to college, Aunt Laura." He was wearing a black T-shirt with the logo of some rock band, and he had a thick silver chain going through the belt loops of his jeans. He went on, "I'm making good money at the restaurant. Dave says in a few months he'll put me on as waiter." Then, with sincere enthusiasm, he added, "Some of the waiters there are like millionaires—they make like a thousand dollars a night."

According to one of Mike's recent emails, Dave, the owner, was someone her sister was with now. He ran a small Mediterranean restaurant on Genesee Street.

"Well, everyone makes their own way," she said. "Just because college was my way doesn't mean it has to be yours." She cleared her throat and pointed to the cookies. As he reached for one, she added, "I'm sure you'll be successful no matter how you get there."

William was going at the cookies. His eyes—and his attention, Laura guessed—shifted from the soundless faces on the television to the voices in the room. Mike wasn't his family. He'd met the boy on only a few occasions. When Laura explained that she wanted to plan the trip so that Mike could get a glimpse of how other people lived, William didn't object. But, she felt, he wasn't exactly enthusiastic either. He didn't offer to show the boy his practice, something Laura would have liked. And there was something else too: the day before Mike arrived, William made a point of putting away all the little valuables he usually left around the house. She tried not to hold this against him. In William's family kids Mike's age were in prep schools, readying themselves for Ivy League educations. He kept a pleasant-enough look on his face, but Laura could tell when he wasn't happy. He hadn't made eye contact with her, for one thing, and most of his answers were just one word.

Every few minutes there was a sound from Mike's phone and he tapped at the buttons again. "Nice, huh," Mike said, turning the phone to Laura to show a picture of his girlfriend Pamela. She had greasy-looking blond hair and a silver hoop going through her right eyebrow. In the picture her head was tipped to the side and her shiny lips were pursed. She wore black makeup on her eyes.

"She's pretty," Laura lied. "How long have you two been seeing each other now?"

"Almost a year. She's all worried this weekend though," he said. He leaned forward but his eyes stayed on the picture. "She thinks I'm gonna find a California girl and cheat. That's why she keeps texting," he went on, a proud bounce in his voice. "She's checkin' up on me."

He leaned back and stretched his long legs. He looked around at the things in the room and set his eyes on William.

"Awesome watch," he said, after a moment, stumbling over to William.

He's outgoing, Laura thought. Maybe he *will* find his way.

"Oh," William said, startled. "Thank you." He crossed his legs and touched the silver. "A gift from your aunt," he said. He looked at the watch adoringly. "Maybe someday you'll have a wife who'll buy you a watch like this," he said, letting his eyes go back to the television.

Mike flashed a quick look at Laura, and she felt her face go hot. William was still wearing his suit, and it occurred to her how Mike must see him: a rich old phony, she guessed. Maybe this wasn't entirely off. He was eighteen years Laura's senior and he did have a tendency toward snobbery.

Once she asked him if he knew the golden rule.

He'd said, without irony, "Everyone does: he who has the gold makes the rules."

Then there was the time she took him to meet her mother. They'd stayed on a pull-out bed because her mother insisted on having them. When she turned out the light on the first night, William laughed before he dozed off. "I never knew you were *white trash*," he'd said.

Her mother told her once, "A relationship is about compromise. You're not going to like *everything* about the person you end up with."

Mama, you were right about that one. There were always things you had to get used to. Benefits of the doubt you had to give. Things you had to pretend not to notice. Things you had to make yourself forget. But she'd never met a man as loyal as William.

"Anything special you want to do while you're here?" she asked her nephew now.

At Venice Beach a man held a sign that said WILL WORK FOR FOOD and begged for conversation, as a woman in a neon wig blew bubbles into people's faces. A dense gray mist hung over the ocean. The air on the boardwalk smelled fresh, save for occasional breezes that carried faint traces of far-off marine life and nearby coconut oil. In a few hours' time, that cool, wet, marine layer would blow in, and the temperature would drop so suddenly and so drastically that you'd need a warm coat—but right now it was shorts weather.

"Look at that graffiti," Mike said, running wildly down the Venice Boardwalk, far ahead, and then running back again to Laura. He was quiet as they walked, but often looked over at her.

When she stopped to take a picture of him, a young woman pushing a stroller with a plastic doll inside asked for spare change. Mike reached into his pocket and gave her the cash from it. The woman said, "Jesus loves you," and walked off.

"How much did you give her?" Laura asked.

"About ten bucks, I guess," he said. "Grandma used to."

People on bicycles flew by like hummingbirds, but their conversations lingered. "Her mother died last week," Laura heard someone say, and the words echoed like death itself. Stray dogs tackled each other wildly in the sand, then carefully chewed away at each other's fleas. Vendors set up card tables and sold their art: mostly beaded necklaces and cartoonish paintings of ocean scenes. The sparkling faces of the starfish wore goofy smiles.

The boardwalk buzzed with loud music from the stores. Mike's squinty eyes gleamed with excitement as they walked. He said, "I've got it, Aunt Laura. I'm going to start a band and rule the world." He held his fists in the air, spun around, and took a dramatic bow. Laura rolled her eyes and grabbed his muscular arm. She felt protective, as if he were young enough to lose in a crowd if she let go.

She had a thought about starting in with him on the importance of going back to school—maybe getting his GED and going to community college for a couple years, then transferring to get his bachelor's degree—but there was something delightful in the boy's smile that made her stop. And she could see, then, in his young mind, in that moment, he was going to start a band and rule the world. And who knew—maybe there was greatness in him.

When they were hungry they got hot dogs from a stand and found a bench near the shore. Mike snapped pictures of the waves coming in and sent them to Pamela. She wrote back something that made him laugh.

"You've had your face in that phone all day," Laura said, pushing his shoulder. "Enjoy the view." She hoped he'd take his time with love, date awhile before making any big decisions. "Seems like things are getting pretty serious," she said, looking at the water.

"Don't worry," he said. "We use protection."

Her face flushed. It hadn't occurred to her that he was having sex already. The last time she saw him, he was playing with action figures. A flicker of something ugly went through her mind: her sister's life. She thought of pregnancy and saw that story unfolding so fast it made her queasy.

"You know," Mike said, "this is the first time I ever saw the ocean." And when he said this, Laura looked at it too, as though she were seeing it for the first time. There was the beauty, yes. But her mind soon went to the things you couldn't see: giant creatures and rip currents that could drag you off without a moment's notice.

He rolled up his jeans and put his feet in the water. She tried it too, for a second, but the water was icy and the salt made her legs sting. She sat down in the sand where the water couldn't reach her and watched him instead. He skipped back and forth in the waves for some time, the way a child would. And there was a strange and desperate loneliness that came to her, seeing him like this—carefree. She was thinking of possibilities, of how different his life might have been if he were hers, and not her sister's.

After a while, he left the shoreline and walked back to where she was sitting on the beach. He was still huffing when he asked her if she trusted him. She told him that, yes, of course she did. "Okay," he said, "then stand up and turn around." He was giddy, still, from meeting the ocean. He stood a few feet away from her. "Come on," he begged, clapping now, "stand up and turn around."

Laura did it.

"Now let yourself fall and I'll catch you."

She hated the thought of this—falling. She could hurt her back. "Really?" she said, in a way that made him know she was hoping to avoid this silly game.

"Come on, Aunt Laura," he said, even more excitedly now. She saw that she had no choice. She took a few deep breaths and tried to fall backward, only she couldn't do it. After a few moments she was finally able to let herself fall toward him. And when she did, he pushed effortlessly with his fingertips at her shoulders, and she bounced up again. She felt exhilarated, buoyant. She'd forgotten the pleasure that could come of these simple acts: letting go, being saved.

"I wanted to say," she said. "I'm always here if—"

"I know, Aunt Laura," he said. "I know you are."

Walking, back to the boardwalk it was quiet except for the crash of waves, the laugh of the seagulls. Mike glanced up at her and let his head tip into his shoulder. "Aunt Laura," he said, "don't you ever want to have kids?"

William was the one who'd made this choice. He'd had two adult children already with his previous wife. Their occasional visits were brief and polite. She knew from the start he did not want more.

"No," Laura said plainly now. People asked her all the time. It was her easiest, her truest lie.

On the boardwalk, two men in a hat shop had shiny suntans and wore their fedoras tipped to the side. When Mike passed one of them, the man dropped a black leather fedora onto the boy's head. "Look at that," the man said to his partner, "it's Johnny Depp."

Mike went to the mirror and gave his reflection a serious stare. Laura could tell from his expression that he believed the man, that he liked what he saw. She didn't. She was surprised that a boy who'd come up the way Mike had didn't have more street smarts.

"Cute," she lied. The hat made him look like the kind of man who'd call out *Hey, Mama* from his car window if he passed you on the street. "Let's get going," she said, taking the hat from his head and handing it back to one of the men. She guided Mike from the store.

With this the men stirred. "Are you gonna let the lady call the shots?" one of them barked. "Never let a lady call the shots."

Mike looked at Laura and laughed and then ran ahead. When she found him in the back of the next shop, he was standing next to a display of glass pipes.

"You can safely stretch an eighth of an inch at a time," the man behind the counter was saying. He had a skull tattooed on his neck, and when his Adam's apple moved, it looked as if the mouth on the skull were talking. Mike pointed at a pair of the earrings and the man set them down on the glass.

"Look at these awesome plugs," Mike said to Laura. "I'll finally be at a full inch."

She looked at him and at the man. "Will they ever go back?" she said.

"Anything over half an inch is what we call 'past the point of no return,'" the man said.

Laura was watching his skull mouth say it. After a moment, she said, "Can't you read? Says right here you have to be eighteen."

The man said, "We have a release form."

"But I'm not his mother."

"Do you really think my mom cares?" Mike said. He touched his earlobes. "She's the one who got me these," he said, looking at the man. The man leaned back on his stool and lowered his eyes.

Laura didn't say anything for a while. Then she said, "It could get infected. And you've said it hurts. Do you want to be in pain the whole time you're here? On the plane home?"

As Mike turned to leave, he knocked one of the earrings onto the floor with his elbow. It rolled under the counter, out of sight.

"Pick it up," the man said, standing.

As Mike went down on his hands and knees to feel under the counter, he muttered, "Asshole."

Laura was relieved the man did not seem to hear. It was then that something gleamed in the sunlight through the opening in his pocket and caught her eye. She understood right away — he'd taken William's watch. She took a few deep breaths and steadied herself with one hand on the counter.

Outside, a pretty blonde sat at a small table. Scribbled on a sign in front of her were the words PSYCHIC READING $10. The woman shuffled her cards and set them down next to the sign. Mike went for her right away.

By the time Laura got there, he was sitting in the chair next to the woman. She could see that he'd already started talking about serious things. She knew it was probably harmless for Mike to have a few minutes with the woman, but it bothered her to think that this strange woman could say things he might remember. Laura walked up beside Mike and gave his shoulder a squeeze. When he looked up at her, she nodded toward the parking lot, which was just a short ways off now. She looked at the woman hard and kept her hand on Mike's shoulder.

"Don't worry," the woman said. Her green eyes looked vacant. "This one's on the house." She shuffled her cards.

Mike looked at Laura for a show of approval. The sun was going down and the cool air was coming in, but the car wasn't very far off. Laura shrugged her shoulders and crossed her arms. She thought of what William would say about the psychic, how he'd never let her hear the end of it if he knew. He'd be getting home soon but could fix his own dinner. She looked away, pretending to pay attention to other things.

Mike and the woman went back to what they were talking about—Pamela. She was planning to attend veterinary school out of state next year, and this had him worried. He was giving details about the relationship, telling the woman things he hadn't shared with Laura. He loved her, for one thing. And he hoped to marry her one day too. Hearing him open up so freely and easily to a stranger made Laura feel dwarfed. Marriage? He was sixteen!

The woman's expression turned serious. She flipped her cards with thought. After a while, "Oh," she said, turning her eyes on the boy. "You'll be together a few months longer," she said, "but then she's going to break it off."

Mike squirmed in the seat. He looked out at the ocean for a moment and then back at the woman. "Can you tell me why?" he said. His voice was different now—harder to hear, but easier for Laura to understand.

"All I know is you're going to do something to ruin it." She was talking in a direct way, and it was easy to see she liked saying these things. She said, "Does your girlfriend get jealous when you talk to other girls?"

Mike told her that, yes, she did, and Laura could see the psychic had gotten to him then. She could see that he wanted more. He leaned in and started going with his questions. He was talking fast, desperate. He was asking the woman all the things he wanted to know. "What's going to happen then?" he asked. "Will there be someone else?" This was something that made him blink hard, something Laura could see he couldn't bear the thought of. And there was more. It came urgently, a child's plea, "What will I be when I get older? What am I going to do?" And one other, last thing he wanted to know about. One other thing he wanted the psychic to tell him. He said, "Will my mom be okay?" And then, "Does it show anything about my mom on there?"

The woman looked pleased when he asked this last thing. A slow smile melted into her cheeks. She rubbed her temple with her fingers and made a show of flipping the big cards onto the little table.

When Laura saw a grim look sweep over her face, she grabbed Mike's hand. "Come on," she said, in a way that made him know she wasn't asking. "Enough now," she said. She shot a severe look in the woman's direction and added, "She doesn't know what she's talking about."

Mike got up and started to walk. "You'll regret losing your Pamela," the woman sang after them.

He pushed the buttons on his cell phone. He said, "I have to call her. I have to let her know."

"Come on, Mike," Laura said. "Calm down. Do you really think that woman can see the future? She's just some junkie with a deck of cards."

He closed his phone and stopped walking. He turned to Laura and his face became red with anger. He said, "Why don't you talk to my mom?"

When she saw his fierce cold eyes on her she gasped. She stopped walking and covered her face with her hands. She did not have an answer. Not for a sixteen-year-old boy. Not for a son. "She's done a lot of things that I don't agree with," she said. "Maybe someday you'll understand."

But his blinking gave him away. He did not understand. He didn't understand some key things about life: how it was a series of choices, and the ones that mattered most were the ones you had to make first. He didn't understand how too late comes too soon. Or that no one can tell you the things you'll regret, the things you won't. And he didn't understand that knowing what's coming doesn't mean knowing how to stop it.

That night the lights of the Ferris wheel on the Santa Monica Pier fizzled like shooting stars as it spun in the California sky. They sat close to each other on the cold metal seat. Laura thought of what happened earlier, before they left the store, when she saw that he'd taken William's watch. A flood of anger made her heart beat fast, and she went to snatch it back from him. But she stopped herself in time.

She'd lose him.

"If you don't let me do it here," he'd said when he stood back up, "I'm just going to do it the second I get home. You know that, right?"

Yes, she knew it. He'd stretch those damn holes as far as they could go. Stretch them until all that was left was a big empty space. Until that tiny bit of skin left on the bottom had torn right in two.

But for tonight there was the sleepy black ocean. It was beautiful, and vast, and wild from way up above. And the waves crashed into the shore in absolute silence. When William asked, she'd say he was never out of her sight. Mike let his hands go over his head when they got to the very top, and Laura did it too. And the people on the pier were nothing more than tiny little blurs, and the cold air felt as if it were made of silk as it slid over their faces. And they went around and around again, each time seeing the starry ocean night anew.

BURGLARY

Carol decided to burglarize her neighbor's house. She was a friend of the family, but there were things she wanted that the family had. She was tired of seeing the things, leaving them for the family. She wore a ski mask and used a flashlight. She went in late at night, when no one was home except the husband. The wife and the kids were out of town visiting with relatives. They would not be back for days, and Carol knew it, so she could take her time getting the things she wanted. Sometimes when the family went away, they left her in charge of the dog, so she had a set of keys that the woman had made for her years ago.

The dog greeted her when she opened the door, its tail wagging. It was a big dog with a dopey disposition—the kind of dog that always seemed to be smiling at his own thoughts. Carol fed it treats from her pocket as she made her way through the house. First she went down the hall to where the children slept. In their room two walls were painted pink, for the little girl, and the other two walls were painted blue, for the little boy. Carol had a gigantic garbage bag. It was the kind of bag you use for things that break through lesser bags. She went to the beds and put all the things that kept the children warm at night into her bag. She took their pillows and their blankets. She took all the stuffed animals that had been tucked underneath the covers. She took the night-light too.

From there she moved into the bedroom that the woman and the man shared. There were things in that room that she wasn't going to leave without. The man was where his wife had left him, tucked underneath the covers of their bed. He didn't say anything to Carol when she came into the room, he just watched. Carol smiled at him and felt relieved when he gave her a nod. The woman's jewelry box was on the dresser, and it was the first thing Carol went to. It was pink, with satin inside. She took the woman's precious things from it. She put the diamond ring on her finger and watched it sparkle in the light. She smiled in the mirror when she saw how it lit her up. She opened the drawers and emptied the silk panties into her bag. She took the nightgowns, and the old flannels too, for when it got cold.

She went into the closet and took the shoes. She took some of the woman's clothes, and then, in the back of the closet, she saw the thing that she wanted most: an old shoebox. Carol had had boxes like this herself, and she had suspected all along that the woman would have one too, but she didn't know it'd be this easy to find. She sat down on the floor and opened it. She started to read through the love notes and cards that the man had written to the woman over the years. There were cards for the woman's birthdays, cards for anniversaries, and cards for Mother's Day—all with special messages in the margins going on about what their love felt like to the man. Then there were pictures of fresh newborn babies, and pictures of the man and the woman going back to when they were very young—at their wedding and holding hands on the beach. Carol touched the pictures and her fingers left marks on the gloss. She dropped the things into her bag, one by one, and when she did it, there was a tickle in her stomach, like when she was in her car going too fast down a hill.

She went over to the man and looked at his pretty face. She wanted to tell him that she was all ready for them to leave, but she had a sense that there was something more in the house, that there were things she hadn't found yet. She went through the house with her flashlight, moving fast now, from room to room, looking for what she might have missed.

She felt something inside her again when she went into the kitchen. There was a smell in the air that had to do with cookies. The woman must have baked cookies before she left. The smell made Carol feel enraged. She knew it was crazy, but the smell was so powerful that she felt she could almost capture it in her hands and put it into her bag. She reached out and grabbed for it, but her hands stayed empty. She thought to try to swallow it. She opened her mouth. She opened the cupboards and smashed the glasses on the shelves. She broke the dishes into tiny pieces. She was so mad; she broke the china. Her hands were bleeding now, but she didn't mind the blood or how it looked on the woman's kitchen floor. She took the leftover lasagna from the fridge and dropped it into her bag. The woman had cooked it for the man before she left so that he would have something good to eat while she was away. She took the pots and the pans so that the woman would not be able to make anything more. She took the spices and the sugar. She took the salt.

She went into the bathroom, and she took the little mirror and put it into the bag.

She went back to the bedroom, where the man was still in the bed. She told him she was ready to go now, and then she folded him up neatly and put him into the bag too, with all the other things. She took the man. She took the father. She took the husband. She took the memories. She took the peace. The things she took were things the family would not be able to get back again, ever.

But the smell was still there. That smell! All around the house the smell was there. It was in every room as she made her way out of the house dragging the heavy bag behind her. It was so sweet and so homemade. She had tasted the woman's cookies before and she knew how good they were. She knew how it made you feel to eat them. You felt the woman's love when you ate them. She wanted to take the smell out of the house once and for all. She wanted to take it from the woman too. She opened all the windows and she opened the doors. She cheered as a breeze came in, hoping it would carry the smell away. The dog ran out into the road and was hit by a car. The car stopped. A woman got out and offered her apologies. She offered to pay the vet bills. But it was too late, the dog was dead.

This was a relief. Carol's bag was full, and it would have been hard to fit the dog anyway.

I'll Go with You

Lillian was at her daughter Susan's house having coffee and banana bread at the kitchen table when Susan's mother-in-law, Jean,
popped by, unannounced, and joined them. Elvis was playing through
the little radio on the kitchen counter, and Jean came in singing along
as if the same song had been on in her car. She plopped herself down
in the chair beside Susan and started to uncoil a few stray curlers from
her hair right there at the kitchen table.

Lillian had known Jean casually when the two of them were
girls. Their families both went to the Assembly of God Church on
Genesee Street. They'd been in the same Sunday-school class for a
few years, that was all. Throughout her life Lillian saw Jean here and
there—at the grocery store or the Sangertown mall—and she was
always polite to her, always taking an extra minute to listen about
whatever was going on in Jean's life. She couldn't say that she didn't
like Jean exactly, just—they were very different kinds of people. Jean
came from West Utica. She'd lived in one of those three-story apartment houses you could see from the Arterial. She'd had five siblings
and her father had left them to fend for themselves. They were just

different kinds of people, that was all. Lillian was shocked when her daughter started dating Jean's son, and even more shocked when, six months after that, the two of them snuck off to the courthouse in downtown Utica and eloped. Now whenever there was a birthday party or a holiday, whenever new people were around who hadn't heard, Jean would get into her elaborate story about how, as children, she and Lillian had been best friends, and how it was so strange and wonderful—a miracle, really—that all these years later their children had met and had fallen in love, and how, now, in their golden years, they got to be grandmothers together.

They did have things in common. The similarities of their lives were nothing short of remarkable, actually. For starters, they looked alike: as kids, both skinny, with frizzy blond hair, icy blue eyes, and noses too large for their faces; and now, in old age, both tall and strong with short white hair. They'd both married at age twenty-one and had both worked as secretaries for the bulk of their lives: Lillian at the high school, and Jean at the life insurance company on Oriskany Boulevard. They'd both had one child, and they both became widows in their fifties. In their sixties, they both had traumatic medical events—Lillian her heart attack, Jean a stroke—that, unbeknownst to them, landed them both in the St. Luke's Rehabilitation Center just behind the hospital, where their children met in the parking lot one frozen January morning.

A few minutes after Jean arrived, another car rattled onto Susan's quiet Marcy street. The snow was coming down hard, whirling about as if it were in a snow globe. The kids had thought they'd have a snow day, and they'd listened to the radio all morning, praying, but the Marcy school district was not one of the names they called out. Susan stood and went to the window. "I don't believe this," she said after a minute, still watching. "That bitch is actually going to flaunt it right under my nose." Susan was seven months pregnant and she'd gained a tremendous amount of weight in a very short amount of time; it took her some effort to sit back down, as if her brain hadn't yet adjusted to her body's new proportions. She took a second slice of banana bread, spread a generous hunk of butter on it, and started to eat. "I should go over there," she said.

Now Lillian got up and went to the window. A young woman, tiny and thin except for the round ball of her giant belly, was waiting at the door across the street. She was a frail thing and looked as if she might be carried off by the wind. When she looked around, Lillian got a glimpse of her face—her hideous face—with its tiny pig nose and miserable frowning lips.

"*That's* her?" Lillian asked her daughter.

"Yes," Susan said. "A real beauty, huh?"

"Oh, my, my," Lillian said. The woman stomped snow from her feet and went into the house, and Lillian came back to the table. She brushed her daughter's head with her hand before sitting back down. "My poor baby," she said. "My poor, poor baby," she said, looking not at Susan, but at Jean. "I can't believe she would have the nerve to come over here like this." She slumped down in her seat, staring at the floor. "Some people just have so much nerve."

Jean was nibbling on her slice of banana bread, avoiding eye contact. She'd stood briefly to peek out the window but sat back down again without going over. After a minute she looked around the room, then went and grabbed the broom from the sliver of space beside the refrigerator, and started sweeping.

"No, Mom," Susan said half-heartedly. "You don't have to do that," she said.

Something inside of Lillian always died when she heard her daughter call Jean Mom. *She* was her mother—no one else. Especially not Jean. She was still here, alive and kicking, thank you very much. She cleared her throat. "Yes, you really don't have to do that, Jean,"

Lillian said. "Sit down." After a minute she added, "I was going to do it later."

"It's not about have to," Jean said, still sweeping. "I'm here. I might as well make myself useful." After a minute she said, "When does Peter get home?"

"Late tonight," Susan said. "Probably seven or eight," she said.

Jean swept the pile of crumbs and dirt into the plastic dustpan. After throwing it away, she sat back down at the table again. She eyed the banana bread for a moment, then stood up. "You know what," she said. "I'm going to go and talk to her." She started putting on her coat. "She doesn't have the right to rub your nose in it like this," she said.

There was an edge in her voice as she spoke, and a flicker of memory came to Lillian—something about Jean's mother screaming—just screaming—at Jean and a few of her siblings in the parking lot of the church. But what was she screaming about? Lillian couldn't recall. She did remember how terrified Jean looked. How she'd shrunk to the size of a child that was three sizes smaller, and the look on her face the next week when Lillian asked her if she was okay. It was the first time she'd seen that emotion—shame—on someone's face, and it left a sort of dent in her brain, a soft spot for Jean. The kids at school told stories about Jean's mother. They said she used to lock Jean and her brothers and sisters in the attic for days on end with no food. They said she had a big bed up there, a supply of water, and a bucket. As a child Lillian didn't pay much attention to such stories, she dismissed them as nonsense, but now, as an adult, knowing all the things she knew about people and what they were capable of, she wasn't so sure. You never knew what went on in someone else's home. You never really knew. It made her shudder to think of it, little Jean locked up in the attic. She stood then, surprising herself. "I'll go with you," she said.

———————

Christmas music was playing when Maria from across the street opened the door. She'd already had her tree up, though Thanksgiving was still a week off. "I want to talk to her," Jean said as soon as Maria opened the door.

"Hello, Jean," Maria said, "Lilly," she said, raising her eyebrows. "I don't want any trouble over here today." She looked at Lillian for a show of understanding, but Lillian looked away. "We're just over here minding our business," Maria went on. "We don't want any trouble. You have a good day now." She started to shut the door, but Jean pushed her elbow in.

"Don't give me that," Jean said. "I know she's here and I'm going to talk to her," she said, peeking into the house. "Where is she?" she said. The girl flashed her face toward the front door as she walked by, then went quickly to the bathroom at the end of the hall and closed the door. "It's okay, honey," Jean called out after her. "We don't bite." She pushed her way past Maria and Lillian followed.

"Jean," Maria said. "I'm going to call the cops if you start anything," Maria said. "I mean it," she said. "I will."

"Now listen to you," Jean said. "We're not going to start anything," she said. "I just want to talk to her woman to woman."

"Your house looks very nice," Lillian said gently, glancing over at the Christmas village that was set up on the picture window. There had to be fifty little cottages, all lit up inside, like a tiny winter town. "With the Christmas decorations, I mean," she said. "Everything looks very nice."

Maria glared at her. "Thank you," she said.

Jean knocked on the bathroom door. "We just want to talk to you, honey," she said. "Woman to woman," she said. "Now come on out of there." She knocked again a few minutes later, and then again a minute after that. "We don't want any trouble," she said. "We just want to talk this over."

At last, the woman opened the door of the tiny bathroom. She had been crying and her face was red. She blew her nose loudly, then looked out at both of the grandmothers. "Peter and I," she said. "We love each other. It might sound crazy to you," she said. "But we do."

Lillian felt something inside her fall to the ground when the woman said this. Up close, she wasn't so ugly. Her features were gentle, actually. Delicate and lovely. Her voice was soft, and something in her tone told Lillian that what she was saying was true.

"Is that right?" Jean said, laughing and looking at Lillian. "That's not what it looks like from over here, honey," she said. "From over here it looks like he's just got himself a little something on the side," she said. "That's all."

Lillian grabbed the woman's hand, pleading. "He has a wife," she said, "my daughter." She pictured her daughter as a young child when she said this, and she felt as if she might start to cry. She cleared her throat and went on. "He has kids. That's a family over there you're breaking up," she said. "Can't you find a man of your own?"

The woman looked at Lillian with what seemed to be genuine compassion. "I'm sorry for your daughter, ma'am," she said. "I am. I really am," she said. "But if it wasn't me, it would be someone else," she said. "He doesn't love her."

"Can't you just get rid of it?" Jean said. "If it's a matter of money," she said, "we can help with that." Her eyes moved briefly to the picture hanging on the bathroom wall, then back to the woman. "I know someone in Syracuse who—"

The woman's tone changed. "Are you crazy, lady?" the woman said. "This is my baby," she said. "It's a girl, if you want to know," she said. "We've named her." She looked at Lillian. "He's going to leave your daughter," she said plainly. "He hasn't told her yet," she said, "but he's going to leave her."

Jean slapped her face then.

The woman looked stunned and afraid. She covered her cheek with her hand and shook her head. "You've got to get out of here now," she said. In a moment, "Get the hell out of here," she screamed.

"I'm calling the police," Maria called out from the kitchen. "I'm going to call the police right now," she said. "I'm calling."

"Look," Jean yelled in her face. "You're going to stay away from my son," she said. "Do you hear me?"

"I'm not staying away from anyone," the woman said with a look of disgust on her face. "We have an apartment together." She waved her fingers in Jean's face, showing her ring. "We're getting married someday," she said. "Didn't you hear?"

The diamond from her ring caught the light and shot rainbows around the room. Lillian felt dizzy, breathless. That son of a bitch had actually given her a ring. A bolt of pain fizzled behind her eye and she felt as if her legs might give out.

Jean and the woman were yelling. Now Jean had shoved the woman, and the woman had fallen onto the floor beside the toilet at an odd and unnatural angle. She was trying to get up, but Jean was over her, yelling. The woman was screaming too. "Get off of me," she was calling out over and over again. She struggled against Jean, but Jean was strong. She was pulling the woman's hair, slapping at her head.

"You're going to leave him alone," Jean was saying. "You hear me," she was saying. "You're going to leave my son alone. Tell me that you can hear me."

A memory came to Lillian, then, from somewhere far off. Susan was three, four years old maybe. It was before her first haircut, when she still had those wonderful ringlets. Those were the best-friend days. The days her daughter would sing her little songs about how she was the greatest mommy in the whole wide world. She thought of brushing her hair. The thousands and thousands of nights she brushed that silky hair, taking care to get every last tangle out. She had brushed her baby teeth twice a day, had tucked her into bed at night and watched her as she fell asleep. All that love she'd given, all that time and care and love, and this was how it turned out: a man who cared so little about her that he got another woman pregnant and planned to leave her like she was nothing, like she was less than nothing, just a bag of garbage in the street. Lillian felt her foot moving. She heard sirens in the distance. No, her foot wasn't just moving, it was kicking. The sirens were getting louder. Her foot was hitting something now. She looked at Jean, whose eyes shot back at her with a mixture of shock and terror, eyes that didn't judge, or regret, or question, eyes that were icy and blue, and very much like her own.

CUSTOMER OF SIZE

Thomas Foster knows that he is a fat man. He and his wife, Eileen
Anderson-Foster, are at the airport checking in for their flight to
Albany when they first hear the term *customer of size*. When the boy behind the counter, Gabe, says it, he uses a soft voice. He says that because
of his size, Thomas may need to purchase a second seat for the flight.
He says that in a minute, he will call a flight attendant over to escort
him onto the plane, so that they can check and see if this will be necessary or not. He says it's policy and that they have to ensure the comfort
of all of their customers. The boy's Thomas can understand. Thomas
does not respond except to tell the boy that it's okay and that he will
go along with it. He takes a seat in the waiting area with his wife.

"Wow," he says to Eileen, "this is a new one, isn't it," he says. "This
has never happened before."

"Don't start with me," Eileen says. "I told you that you needed
to do something," she says. "And now look." She puts her back to
him and then opens her book. When a flight attendant comes to the
gate a few minutes later, Eileen walks to the bathroom. She does not
turn around.

Gabe talks to the girl in her ear and then points his finger over at Thomas. The two of them nod their heads. "Mr. Foster," Gabe calls out from behind the counter in a minute, "we're all set."

Thomas straightens his suit and tie before he makes his way over. He walks like he knows people are watching. He extends his hand to the girl, who is a pretty young thing, and he gives her a firm shake. Gabe introduces her as Joyce. When she greets him she says, "You're my first customer of size, Mr. Foster," with a big smile, like she's won something.

"Well," Thomas says, "fancy that," smiling back. "You're the first flight attendant who says I'm too fat," he tells her, grinning. His voice is precise. "So I guess we're even." He looks up at Gabe, whose face has become bright red. He is fussing with some papers on the counter, and Thomas says, "Well, the first or the second, anyway."

Joyce lets out a giggle and starts walking toward the plane. "Follow me," she says, and then she makes a point of turning around and waving her fingers at Gabe. There is something playful about the way she does it, and it makes Thomas wonder what's between them. Gabe gets a goofy smile on his face and waves to her. When Thomas looks over at him, Gabe's eyes dart back to his papers. It is quiet for a minute, and then Joyce says as they walk, "So, what is it that you do for a living, Mr. Foster?"

Thomas takes a second. Girls like Joyce don't talk with him. He wants to get the tone right. "Oh, dear," he says. "You wouldn't believe me if I told you."

"Come on," she says. "Try me."

"Okay," and then feeling clever, he adds, "but I will not tolerate any laughs out of you, young lady." He shakes his finger at the girl and says, "Under no circumstances can you laugh. Understood?"

"Understood," Joyce says with a nod and a smile. She opens the door of the plane and lets Thomas move down the aisle in front of her.

She rests her hand on his back as he passes. An older flight attendant, who is checking things here and there in first class, looks at both of them for a time and then looks away without saying anything.

"Okay," he says to Joyce as they make their way to the second part of the plane, "I'm a professional wrestler," he says, looking back at her. "You've heard of *The Tornado*, right?" he says.

Joyce scrunches up her face. For a minute, she cannot tell if this is a joke. When she catches Thomas's eye and sees a little squint, she laughs.

He says, "Oh, all right. You've got me. I sell Bibles for a living. From door to door."

"Come on," she says, laughing again. "What do you do really?" she begs.

"No. No," he says, turning red. "That one is no joke." Right away he adds, "Do you have a Bible, dear?"

Joyce says, "Oh. I'm sorry." Then she says, "Yes. I have a Bible—I think I do, at least. I haven't heard of door-to-door in a while though, that's all." She directs him toward the first seat in coach. She says, "Here you go, Mr. Foster. Try this one on for size," and when she says this, she winks and pats his shoulder with care.

"I wasn't always this fat, you know," he tells her, "I had my day." He then lowers himself into the wide open seat. "Ta da," he says, holding his palms up in the air. "See that? Didn't I tell you this was going to be a breeze?" he says.

"Hey," she says. "There's nothing wrong with it. I'd be bigger myself if it wasn't for this job," she says. "They weigh us, you know— it's a nightmare really," she tells him. Then, "So far so good, Mr. Foster. But we still have a few things to check." She reaches over his lap for the seat belt.

"Let me," he says. He tugs at the metal piece with one hand and carefully guides all the fabric out with his other hand. He pulls the fabric over his lap and says, "You see. Everything is going to be fine." He presses the two pieces together but there is no click. He keeps his hand over it and then smiles up at Joyce.

"Mr. Foster," she says. "I don't think I heard any click. Can you move your hand for a second so I can get a look?"

Thomas lets go, and the belt falls loose on his lap. "Let me give it another try," he says. This time he sits straight up and holds his stomach in. He yanks at the fabric, and then, in a second, the belt clicks together.

"Okay," Joyce says, "That'll work out all right, I suppose. Now just one more thing," she says. She leans over him and starts to push at the armrest. Thomas lifts his arms over his head to make it easier for her to do it. She moves the armrest a bit, but then sees that she is pressing it into his flesh, and she notices that his body is taking up a bit of the next seat too.

"Mr. Foster," she says. "I'm sorry, but I'm afraid we have a problem here. Both armrests have to be able to go down all the way."

Thomas forces at the armrest for a while, but he can't get it to go down. He takes some breaths and lets his eyes close for a minute. It is clear to Joyce that he is done making jokes. She watches him undo the seat belt, and she tries to think of something to say. When she opens her mouth to offer her words, she notices that Thomas can't make the armrest move back up again either. "Dear. Oh, will you look at this now," he says. "Now how do you like this?" He sighs, then, "Can you do me a favor, dear?" He raises his arms in the air again, "Can you give it a try for me?"

Joyce pulls at the armrest but it won't go. She moves in front of him and gives it a push from that angle, and then she tries it from the other side too. "Oh, Mr. Foster," she says. "I can't get it to budge," she says. "I'll have to go and get Gabe, or else someone from security— they'd be better at this."

"No," he says, "that won't be necessary." He pulls at the armrest some more. He squirms about this way and that, but he is fixed in his place. "Just get my wife," he says. "I'm sure she can help me with this. She's done it before, you know."

"Of course," Joyce says.

As she turns and starts to walk off, Thomas says in a soft voice, "I hope you won't look down on me, dear," he says. "I'm trying."

Joyce hears him. She closes her eyes, but she does not turn around or stop walking. She leaves the plane and walks over to the counter where Gabe is standing. The waiting area has filled up, and there is a line now.

Eileen is eyeing two young boys who are running around the terminal as their mother reads from a tabloid when she sees Joyce walking over to the counter. She watches her lean in close to Gabe and talk for a minute. She sees the smile form on Gabe's face and watches as they both have a laugh together. She knows it has to do with Thomas. In a minute, when Gabe calls her name over his speaker, Eileen follows Joyce onto the plane.

"Oh. Perfect," she says when she sees Thomas in his seat. "Look at him now," she says. "He's stuck."

"Come on, honey," Thomas says. "Please. It's not the time now," and then "Just be quiet and off to it," he tells her.

Eileen shakes her head back and forth. She stares at him for a while, and then she gets this look on her face. She leans in close, as if she is going to kiss him, but instead she says, "Fatty, fatty, two-by-four. You can't fit through the kitchen door." She moves her head around in this way when she says it, and she gets to laughing really hard. She looks over to Joyce for a laugh—as if they are in agreement here.

Joyce turns away. She says, "I tried to pull the armrest up myself, but I couldn't manage it." And then, "He said you've helped him with this sort of thing before."

Eileen stops smiling and glares at her husband. "Yes," she says, "with this sort of thing." She seems to be contemplating something, and Joyce is not sure what will happen next. After a few minutes of standing there, Eileen steps over Thomas's feet and sits down in the window seat next to him. She turns her body so that she is facing him. She puts her feet up against his middle, and she says, "Now lift your arms, Fat Boy," and then she forces her feet into different parts of his stomach.

"Christ," Thomas says, "your heels."

"You be quiet," she tells him, and then she looks at Joyce, pointing to the armrest with her free hand. She says, "Now give it a try."

Joyce pulls at the armrest but it doesn't move. Eileen presses her feet deeper into her husband's flesh, and Thomas lets out a whimper. Joyce gives the armrest another try, and this time it goes up.

Thomas does not say anything for a while. He just sits there. He looks at the floor. He seems smaller to Joyce, next to his wife. After a time, he stands up and wipes some sweat from his forehead with his sleeve. Joyce notices all the shoe prints on his jacket. Something big is going to happen here, she thinks. But Thomas just leans over to his wife and kisses her on her forehead in this really gentle way. He looks at her in the face for a while. Neither one of them says anything.

That night, for the first time in a while, Joyce goes straight home after work. She puts her son in his little bed early, and then she looks through her bookcase and finds her Bible. She puts it on her bedside table and opens it. She reads a few lines from the page she opens to, and then she does up a nice dinner for her husband. She is careful about how much gravy she puts on his meat, and she does not use butter with the mashed potatoes. In bed, she tells him about it. She tells him about how fat the man was, and about how he sells Bibles, from door to door. She tells him about how the man was stuck and about how his wife kicked at him right in his middle. She tells him about all the nasty things the woman said and how when it was all finished, she thought there was going to be some big fight. She'd thought she'd have to call security to break it up, but then instead, the man just gave his wife this really gentle kiss on her forehead. And she tells him how it made her want to cry when she saw it, when she saw him forgive her.

RECESS

My hand is resting on her lap, and there's a breeze this afternoon. She's telling me how our son put Spider-Man Band-Aids on all of his old wounds. I watch her mouth, thinking of when she was younger, just mine, before any of this. She's always moved her mouth in that same funny way. We used to go to this place called the Frog Pond—all the rooms had frogs for decorations. In the black of night the ceiling would glow with bright stars. In June she starts chemotherapy. The doctors say I should be optimistic, but I don't feel particularly optimistic. We love knowing it will end. She stops talking and asks me what's wrong, and I tell her it's nothing. She leans closer; I meet her halfway; we kiss. We are locked in this moment of waiting, like children running wild at recess.

THE CORRECT WAY TO BREATHE

Tessie is new this month and sits beside me in the circle. Petite, with a worn look, she keeps her mittens on throughout the two-hour meeting. It's the middle of summer, but no one asks about the mittens. We understand sometimes, air hurts.

There are fourteen of us in the group, all women. We meet on the first Saturday of every month in the lobby of the old church on Washington Avenue near Downtown Crossing.

"Did you know the average pain patient usually sees six doctors before getting a proper diagnosis?" Dr. Flores says, scanning the room with her kind, expressive eyes.

"I had an easier time finding a husband," says Tessie.

Everyone laughs.

We talk about how we all get crushes when we find someone who says he can help.

In his office I wear my pink gown. It's made of paper and it opens in the back. My legs dangle from the paper-covered exam table like a child's as I read the articles about him that hang on the wood walls, study his Ivy League degrees. Prescription brochures promise a better life and there are the muffled sounds of his laughter from Exam Room B.

When he comes into the room a few minutes later he is singing the song with my name in it again. He is a tall man with mostly gray hair, a straight nose, and a clean-shaven face. His dark brows and thick lashes highlight the playfulness in his eyes. He tells me the song is a real song, from Dylan, from the '60s. I think: *Bedside manner, my ass, a girl can take only so much charm.*

I pretend not to love it.

I wonder if he sings to all of his patients. I think: *Maybe I'm his favorite patient, his wittiest patient, his* something. For appointments I try to look pretty, but not like I tried to look pretty. I think: *If he likes me, maybe he'll try harder to fix me.*

His resident enters the room a moment later. "This is Dr. Kinsley," he says, "my good fellow," and squeezes the younger man's shoulder. Dr. Kinsley seems to be about my age—not yet thirty—but looks like a child dressed for Halloween. His white coat is too big; his glasses sit crookedly on his nose.

My doctor is careful when he handles my bare foot. Resting it in the palm of his hand, he says to Dr. Kinsley, "Allodynia, hyperalgesia, edema, thermographic changes?"

Dr. Kinsley looks confused. He reaches for my foot, and my leg jumps, nearly hitting my doctor in the one place it shouldn't.

"Careful," my doctor says to both of us. He goes on, "Notice how red the feet are? Hot to the touch. See that mottling on the legs?" He adds, "And when do we see piloerection like this?"

The young man lights. "Fight or flight?" he says unsteadily.

"So?"

"CRPS," Dr. Kinsley says. He fixes his glasses and says the rest of what he knows: how it involves a malfunction of the sympathetic nervous system; how it usually occurs following a surgery or trauma; and how, here, the body changes so the nerves interpret everything—touch, temperature, vibration, sound—as pain.

My doctor asks, "And where does it come in on McGill?"

Dr. Kinsley looks at me with newfound interest. "First?"

"Yes," my doctor tells him. "Forty-two," he says. "The very top of the pain scale. Amputation of a digit is next at thirty-nine. Toothache is eighteen."

"Can you tell him what a forty-two feels like?" my doctor asks me.

I try. The words I choose are from the pain questionnaire that I fill out before appointments. The words I choose are always the same. I say, "Punishing, sickening, fearful, cruel." I say, "Burning, gnawing, searing, dull. Continuous," I say.

I leave my cane on the table for the demonstration. Bare feet, toes curled, I whimper. Ten steps forward. Ten steps back.

"I'm sorry," my doctor says, "I know that's difficult. But you're lucky," he says. "At least we know where the damage is."

I think of the vast spectrum of that word—*lucky*. How we let it mean so many things.

I get myself back up on the table, allow him to manipulate my legs. He's checking for signs of spread. What started in my right foot has spread to my left. *Mirroring*, was how it was explained to me.

"Does this hurt?" he asks. "This? This? This?"

"No. No. Not really," I say.

"Not really," he repeats to Dr. Kinsley. "That's important. Anything that isn't a no is a yes," he says.

Now he wants to test my reflexes. Only he can't find the instrument he needs to do it. He starts singing the Peter, Paul and Mary song "If I Had a Hammer," until Dr. Kinsley gets the hint.

He reminds me of my father. Not the one I had, the one I wanted.

———————

At home, I teach my terrier, Stella, new tricks. In the last few months we have mastered the basics—*sit, down, speak, off, give me your paw*—and now we're onto more complicated things. Last week I taught her *kiss.* A smack of my lips, and now she runs to me and bumps her matte black lips to mine.

The hardest trick to teach is *stay.*

Months of practice have brought us nowhere. First, *sit.* Then: hand flat, palm in her direction, and one small step back. When she doesn't move, I say, "Good stay," in a soft voice, and give her a bit of freeze-dried liver. I circle her at this distance and she follows me with her eyes, turns her head when I'm behind her, but keeps her butt planted on the ground. "Good stay. Good stay," I say, palm still flat at her.

But six inches is the absolute range of her commitment. Another step back and she's at my side.

Where's my treat? She seems to want to know.

When my husband comes home from work I show him our latest: *roll over.* First, *down.* Then, freeze-dried liver ready, I rotate my hand in a half-circle in front of her nose.

"Roll over," I say, "Roll over." After a few tries her body does a swift flip.

But my husband's eyes never leave today's envelopes. "That's great," he says.

A little while later and I have two basins of water going—one warm, one cold—and I'm giving my feet a few agonizing minutes in each. Cold is razor blades. Warm is lava. This is one of the desensitization techniques the doctor suggested.

I tell my husband what he said. How he called it boot camp. How he said he can "get me my life back." There will be a series of nerve blocks in my spine, and after that, ketamine infusions. I'll go to neuro-biofeedback and physical therapy every day.

"Ketamine?" My husband perks up. "You mean like LSD?"

"It's experimental," I say. I've never used drugs, and I try not to let on how much this scares me. "He said they're sending people to Germany for it. They put you in a coma for a week, and in the quiet time, your body sort of *forgets* the pain." When he doesn't say anything I add, "He said they wake up pain-free." Then, "These are the absolute worst cases. *Full-body* cases."

I go on. "Anyway, they use lower doses here—you don't quite enter a coma. But he says he's seen really good results."

My husband keeps looking at the side of the room where I'm not. He doesn't say anything. Two years ago, when he said for better or worse, I know he meant it. But what he was counting on was having some of both. Like any good nurse, he's learned the way to let his heart go hard. He's quiet, now, when I cry, but he always picks me up on time.

He leaves the room. Fifteen minutes later he's back with his laptop. Noises tell me he has mail.

"Did I tell you Becca's pregnant again?" he asks.

"Yes."

"Their second already," he says.

Neither one of us talks. Finally, "Dave must be happy," I say.

"I guess," he says. "Worried about money."

"Why would *Dave* worry about money?"

Desensitization technique two: textures. I have silk, denim, tweed, corduroy, lace, and something that feels like, but is not, fur. I've put the fabrics in a wicker basket that Stella believes is a special nest just for her. One by one I slide them out from under her sleeping body, and work them over my feet as she snores.

"Well, because Becca will probably be out of work for a while again, that's why."

The reality show where people have to stay locked in a house for three months comes on, and the beauty queen is *freaking out* on the thug. She's just chest-bumped him! We're hooked. When the show is finished, my husband has a call to make in the other room. He hands me the remote control and a blanket from the back of his chair.

"Here," he says, leaving it next to me. "You look cold."

But the blanket weighs a thousand pounds.

And I wonder how one thing can be so heavy for one person and so light for someone else.

They say dogs can't read facial expressions, but I say *they* can't read dogs. My smile sends Stella running for a toy. And when I cry my tears never make it so far as my chin.

At group Tessie is learning the power of denial. Like the rest of us did when we got diagnosed, she's going from doctor to doctor for *second* second opinions. What she wants is a better disease.

I tell her about my aunt, the one who died of breast cancer. How even after surgery, and months of chemotherapy, she kept thinking the doctor was going to call, say there'd been a mistake.

Tessie looks at me with something like understanding. But after a moment she asks what the autopsy showed.

At the next appointment the doctor leads me through the main office and into his private office. It's like we're old friends, the doctor and I. We sit on opposite sides of his leather wraparound. The hospital is next to the college and for a few moments we watch the students pass carrying their heavy books and easy dreams, oblivious to what waits next door.

The doctor sinks into the cushions, lets his knees fall apart. He likes to start with small talk, and in this way we've come to know certain things about each other. He knows that I'm married, that before I injured my foot, I worked as a photographer's assistant. He knows that I wanted to be a mother. I know that he's on his second wife, that though he's fifty-seven, he just welcomed his second son. I know that he travels for conferences, makes a lot of money, but most of the time, he feels spent.

Once he talked to me about what it was like, being a surgeon, always having that closer view. How sometimes, whether he's driving his car on the highway, or helping his sons into bed at night, it strikes him how fragile we are, how breakable.

But usually we find common ground. New York, for one thing. We both started in New York. "Did I ever tell you about my mom," he says, "how she used to have me swimming in the Hudson when I was a kid?" He gets to laughing about this and when he does, the top of his mouth goes over the bottom just the way Warren Beatty does it. He says, "You know the Beach Boys song 'Surfin' USA'? Well, when they got to the part about Manhattan Beach, I used to think they were talking about the Hudson." His face goes red. He is a man anyone would want to kiss. Good, even wrinkles. A kind man's wrinkles. Old joys lit by new. I know that in a minute we will get back to who we are, doctor and patient, but for now, we could be anyone.

"It all comes down to one question," he says at last. "How can we minimize the pain?"

"It's important to be prepared for bad days," Dr. Flores is telling the group. She wants us to get dressed every day. She wants us to wear makeup. "Looking better means feeling better," she says.

"That explains a lot," says Tessie.

Everyone laughs.

My mind goes to my father. Age eleven, and I'd get into my sister's makeup bag, put eyeliner on, before his visits. I used to think that if he saw me like that—with big, beautiful eyes—he'd come by more. But he never did, even though he lived the next town over.

After group I mention this to Dr. Flores. "He nothinged you," she tells me. Saying it's the worst way to hurt a child, to make them feel like they just don't mean much. She says that by some accounts children who are ignored are worse off than children who are abused.

You don't know what you've lost until you see someone who has it. When my doctor returns from his two-week vacation in Australia, it's time to begin the series of nerve blocks, and Vickie, the pretty nurse, is my nurse the first day. She wears cotton-candy-pink scrubs and her long, dark hair in a high ponytail. An old man on the other side of the curtain has just proposed to her.

Her smile's not yet faded when she gets to me, Velcros a blood-pressure cuff around my arm.

"Pretty earrings," I say to her diamonds.

"Oh, these," she says. "They're from engagement rings," she says. She plinks my forearm until veins swell. "Hold your breath on three," she says, and sticks me on *two*.

Dr. Kinsley comes over, scribbles something on my paperwork.

She stands beside him, looks at her watch, and writes something down. She says, "Must be hard on you, these patients. A tough disease."

"Counting my days," he says. Then, looking at me, he says, "I mean—I don't plan to specialize in pain management." He clears his throat, looks at the papers, and asks, "On a scale of one to ten, ten being the worst pain you've ever been in, where would you rate your pain right now?"

"Ten," I say. The weight of a sheet would be crushing, and the stir from the cool air vent is making my heart pound.

He writes something down. "Has anyone gone over the risks?"

"No."

"Basically, there's nerve damage, paralysis, and—it's very rare, but we have to say it—death."

I close my eyes.

He adds, "Really, it's very rare that anything should happen. You'll be fine." He hands me the clipboard and the pen. "Right here," he says. "Next to the *X*."

"When did you last eat or drink anything?" Vickie asks.

"Last night around ten."

"Any allergies?"

"No."

"Any contacts, dentures, or hearing aids in?"

"No."

"And who's driving you home today?"

"My husband."

"He's in the waiting room?"

"No. He's—can you call him when I'm done?" I ask. When she frowns I add, "He had to work."

My doctor arrives and comes to my bed.

"Look who's back," Vickie says, squeezing his shoulder. "How was it?"

"Wonderful," he says. "I got to spend a lot of time with my boys." He gets to talking about the Great Barrier Reef.

As he talks I watch the green line on my heart monitor rise and fall and imagine the turquoise mountains of soft water that I know from other people's photographs. I see the doctor bouncing in them, pulling sparkling things up from the bottom of the ocean for his boys to look at as they patrol the shoreline, chase menacing waves back out into the sea. *But, Doctor*, I think. *How could you take a vacation from our disease? Take me, next time. Take me away from it too.*

In a few minutes I'm prone in the icy white operating room. A team of radiologists, surgical nurses, anesthesiologists, and residents surround me. Heavy lead smocks cover them, neck to knee.

Open gown, I am naked.

No one looks but everyone sees.

On the fluoroscopy machine my spine is a star.

My doctor asks Dr. Kinsley, "What are the three most important things to remember about this procedure?"

Dr. Kinsley is silent.

"Position of the patient. Position of the patient. Position of the patient," my doctor says, maneuvering the wedge that's under my stomach.

The surgical cap covers his gray hair and in this light he looks younger. He says to me, "Now, you remember what I told you about FDR? You have nothing to fear but fear itself."

"I was afraid you were going to say that, Doctor," I tell him.

After a moment, "No pun intended?" he says.

His too-smooth gloved hands rub a yellow liquid over my lower back. And then there's a terrible boring ache—like a tooth-ache—deep in my spine as he weaves his giant needles between my vertebrae.

Position of the patient: *This wasn't supposed to be my life.*

A hand rubs my clenched fist. Someone else is petting my leg.

"Hold still," my doctor says. "Hold still." But he is saying this for himself. I am strapped down to the table. My nerves drink his medicine. It's when the pain is gone that I feel how bad it was.

"Everything is going to change for you now," Dr. Kinsley says.

But somehow him saying this makes me understand that it won't.

In recovery Vickie brings me chocolate-chip cookies and cranberry juice. She stays with me, tells me things about her life that I won't recall. She's nice, *too.* And I know, then: I am no longer like her. By this, I don't mean I am no longer young like her, or pretty like her. I mean: I am no longer *human* like her.

In neurobiofeedback, the therapist tells me the correct way to breathe. "In through your nose, slow and deep, let your belly rise, and then let it all come out through your mouth for five," she says.

Electrodes measure my brain waves as I watch a Pac-Man on a TV screen. In her soft voice, she tells me to think of a time when I was stronger, remember a place that's mine and mine alone.

I think back to when I first moved to Boston. I was going to school for photography. I'm so excited to try my new camera lens that I cut class, walk forty minutes from my apartment in the North End to the Public Garden.

I walk without using a cane.

An old woman on the other side of the pond. Her long aqua coat. Her hair is done in a loose white bun. Every few minutes she extends her arm, releases a handful of seeds onto the water. The ducks cheer when she lets go.

Sunlit afternoon, the trees rain their leaves. Red and orange and yellow drip from their branches. On the glassy surface of the pond the weeping willows blur and heal, blur and heal. Tiny voices of tiny birds bounce through the air. And I know things will never be the same again. Not just this way again.

I am thinking about what makes a person come to a park in the middle of the afternoon and feed the ducks by herself. To think of this calms me, slows my eager blood. Soon I know again: more time, there's more time.

Then the picture I've been waiting for—the woman's stretched arm, the swan's open wings. This could be magic. White feathers, and I wonder what it'd be like to slow-dance with the doctor. Here, in this park with this kind old woman, these generous living things. I wonder about resting my head on his sturdy chest, hearing him hum something—anything—in my ear. I wonder how he'd look at me if my gown were made of silk, not paper.

A rainbow appears on my computer screen. The therapist's nurturing voice. She wears pastel sweaters, corduroys. "Good girl," she tells me.

When I return to the hospital for the final nerve block, the doctor is feeling playful. He says, "This isn't going to be comfortable," and he rolls a towel and places it under the wings of my back. My head falls backward and, positioning me, he shifts it around in a not-so-nice way.

"Ouch," I say, and glare. We are so close; his face is just ten inches away from mine.

He's smiling. "Oh," he says. "Did I hurt you?" he says, and he moves my head very carefully. "Is that better?"

And I say, not knowing what I mean, "It could be."

Then he takes both of his big hands and does this thing. It's a thing I know I will always think about, that will always leave me wanting more, please—somehow, make it happen again, go back. He rubs his hands all over my face in a playful but tender, gentle way. The gesture is at once something you would do to a small child whom you love dearly and something tender you would do to a lover whom you love dearly.

The doctor is over me, and he says, "If you were one of my kids"— he stops for a moment—"I'd kiss you right now." To the nurses and Dr. Kinsley he says, "It's amazing how one little kiss can take away the pain."

Love is silent. The doctor cannot know that anything has changed in the doctor-patient relationship. Cannot know there is something else there inside me, in the places he is sticking his needles, trying so desperately to fix.

He puts the gigantic needle into my spine, and his arm rests half over my breast, half over my heart. *Something is happening inside of me, Doctor,* I want to say. "Stay still," he tells me, "or I'll start singing again." The others laugh. They joke along, "Please, don't move." But I wouldn't dream of moving. Not now. Not when his arm is where it is—resting over my heart like this.

A drug called Versed causes amnesia, makes it so I will not have flashbacks of the things I hallucinate, and I do not remember much from the week I spent in the hospital having ketamine infusions. Some things stay.

The nurse's gigantic melting face. Her eyes dripping to where her lips should be. My hand is the size of an infant's hand. Cannot move. Cannot talk. The music is playing in slow motion. Everything is in slow motion. Foam in my mouth—someone help! Spinning bed, sinking down, down. Throwing up. Was my whole life a dream? These wrinkles! I am one hundred years old. Oh, God. How long have I been here?

When I come to, my doctor is not there. I keep my lipstick fresh just in case. Struggle to remember my lost week.

At group I tell the women about my progress. After all the treatments the pain that used to be a ten is a four. They marvel. I do too, though it's uncertain how long the relief will last.

Before we leave, Trish speaks up. It's clear from the darkness under her eyes that she's not slept in days. "Have any of you ever thought of just ending it?" she asks.

We look down at our shoes. We give what we have, and what we have are clichés.

Someone says, "Everything happens for a reason."

"Everything?" Tessie asks.

Someone says, "That which doesn't break you only makes you stronger."

"Isn't there a point of strong enough?"

Dr. Flores wants her to think in practical terms. She says, "It may not seem like it, but pain is a good thing. It lets you know when there's damage. It lets you know when damage is coming."

I think of the Latin word it comes from, *poena*: it means punishment. I stay quiet.

Tessie says, "I feel like I'm just trying to get through the days."

Brenda's white hair is wound in a tight bun. Looking at her, I'm reminded of how easy it is to see what's missing and not what's there. Her southern accent comes alive when she's mad. "Honey," she says, resting her leathery hand in the place where her leg isn't. "It's not so different from what anyone else is doing."

On the way out I stop Tessie. "I've thought of it," I say. I picture my feet blue-black to the ankles, the way they used to be.

Her eyes take the shine of relief.

I tell her, "You learn to live with it." And when I say this, I realize—*you do*. And I feel amazed, then, at how much we can endure, at how resilient we really are.

"No," Tessie says. "I can't. I won't."

"You can," I say. "You will."

My husband has taken to going to the gym. There are muscles now where soft places used to be.

I show him Stella's latest. When I pull the trigger on my finger-gun she drops to her side and holds that position for a few beats.

He laughs. When she pops up, he tries it himself. "Play dead," he says, the way I did. She goes down again, the whites of her eyes flashing.

"That's the best thing I ever saw," he says. "How about we take her to the park on Sunday?"

It's been years. "I'd love that," I say.

At a follow-up appointment the doctor meets me in the waiting room. A point of his finger and I follow him to his office. He closes the door and goes with the song for a few lines.

My heart sings.

"How's my favorite patient?" he says, as he sits down next to me.

There's the usual small talk. I tell him I'm thinking of going back to school, he says something about his new house, and then we move on to the details about how I've been feeling.

When the appointment is over he stands up. "Of course you can call me if you have any problems," he says, "but I don't expect we'll be seeing each other again."

My heart sinks.

He goes for the door.

Doctor, stay.

But I say nothing. And the doctor, he just leaves.

At the receptionist's desk he turns to me and says my full name. He extends his hand and gives me an ordinary shake, but lets our hands fall below the counter where no one can see. And something happens, then—a squeeze.

I look at him, but he does not look back at me. He just holds on.

ROYALTY

S he's saying, "Well, she comes up to me at night and begs. That's how I know."

"Maybe she just wants something to eat," I say. "Did you try playing with her? I remember her always with that damn rope, wanting someone to pull on it."

"No," she says. "I know hungry. Hungry is a kiss on the mouth. Play is her chest to the ground. When she's scared she tucks her tail between her legs. For outside, she goes in circles.

"This is different—this look on her face, it's something I've never seen, you know, and I can tell what she wants. She's asking me about it, she wants to know—*where is he?* She wants me to explain. I try. I say, 'Daisy, he's gone.' I tell her he's not coming home—that he's dead. But this is too much for her. She can't swallow 'never again.' Those eyes on me at night—her paws stretched up on the couch, like she thinks I've forgotten something, and it's her job to remind me."

I'm quiet.

She says, "You awake?"

"Of course," I say, used to her late-night calls.

"If she keeps up like this, I don't know what I'll do. It's hard enough to keep it together in this apartment. Goodwill only takes the clothes. And this look she's giving me. I understand it all too well. I want someone to give *me* answers."

"I wish I could have stayed longer," I say. "If you need me, I'll—"

"They say dogs don't have a sense of time. Maybe that's it. Maybe for her it's like he just left. Or maybe she's been waiting a hundred years."

"She's young," I say. "It's the old dog who can't learn, right?"

"In dog years she's my age. Eight already. You expect twelve to fifteen will be a lifetime, but when you have one you learn: dog years go by fast. I remember when we first got her, an old lady on the street told me to enjoy her, like she knew it'd be over in the blink of an eye."

Then she says, "Did I tell you what she does when I take her out now? She pulls at her leash like when there's a squirrel. Only, there's nothing! She gives the look here too, after a few blocks, *This way?* I can't blame her for trying. I carry her home." She says, "I've even had to buy one of those dog strollers like you see people using so I can get her around the city with me."

"The way it used to be," she says, "we would take her with us on all of our trips. In London they knew our names at the theater. Those days we were everywhere, not a care in the world. In Paris, they would serve her filet mignon on china beneath the table. They called her Princess Daisy, and we'd laugh—calling each other Queen, calling each other King."

THE GOODBYE PROCESS

It wasn't that Eleanor didn't have friends, but in her later life, even long before she was sick, most of them stopped coming around the way they used to, and her husband, Richard, not blind, noticed this. He started to calculate a strange sort of list, sitting there at the hospital in those last few weeks, Eleanor in and out of consciousness—he was wondering who would come to her wake, to her funeral. As it was they both came from smaller families. The kids had had a lot of friends during high school, but all those people had moved away for college, and then made their lives somewhere else. Of his own friends—*Could it be that he had made so few in their life together?*—many had already died. Those who hadn't had moved to Florida. There would be some stragglers, Richard was sure, that he wasn't thinking of. Eleanor's childhood friends, if they saw the newspaper. And there were her sisters, their families. Still, he'd been to calling hours where there were lines at the casket. At his brother's funeral, he recalled, a young man from the local coffee shop came with a tearful story about how his brother had given him a bit of advice at the cash register that had set his life on track, made a difference. Eleanor deserved a line, some pathetic mourners.

"What happens if only a few people come," Richard had asked the funeral director, Tony, a large man with a big stomach and thinning hair. This was the day after Eleanor died. They were walking into Tony's office at the funeral home. On one of the walls an unsettling display: the back quarter of at least twenty different caskets. Richard quickly picked the one he thought Eleanor would like—oak, with a cream velvet interior—then he positioned himself at the mahogany dining table in the center of the room with his back to the casket wall. He cleared his throat and went on. "We're older, I mean. There's not many people who—"

Tony closed his eyes for a moment and nodded his head as if he'd heard this question before. Something in his face set Richard at ease. "You could do the funeral service here," he said, "right after the wake." He was fingering through the life insurance papers as he spoke, making eye contact every few seconds. "That's what most people do nowadays," he said.

"Not at the church?" Richard said. "I don't know."

"We have pews in the main parlor, Mr. Cardinal," Tony said. "People find it to be a very spiritual place," he said. He handed Richard a paper to sign, reaching over the table and pointing at the correct line even though it was highlighted and marked with an X. "If you're worried about filling two separate services," he said, "this would help."

Richard closed his eyes and took a breath. He'd always let Eleanor make the decisions, and he wished that he could ask her what to do now. It occurred to him that she—Eleanor, Eleanor's body—was there somewhere in another room of the funeral home already. He felt almost comforted by this.

"Did you say that she went to the Assembly of God?" Tony said.

"Yes," Richard said. "That's right." A wave of shame washed over him; he'd always let her go to church alone.

"Pastor Pat could do the funeral service," Tony said. "He's here all the time. He was just here last week," he said.

The room was quiet. Richard rested his forehead on his hand. He'd been dreading getting through two days, and he felt something softening within his chest. "Okay, then," he said. "Let's do it that way," he said. "If Pastor Pat can come—"

"You know, Mr. Cardinal," Tony said, leaning away. He crossed his legs and looked at Richard as though he were trying to figure something out. "There is one other thing," he said. "This isn't something I usually bring up, and it wouldn't solve your numbers problem," he said.

"Go ahead," Richard said. "I'm listening."

"There's someone you can call if you wanted," Tony said. "A woman. A professional. She might be able to," he said, drawing out the word *to* for a while, then he went on, "help things along," he said at last.

"Help things along?" Richard said.

"Well, this is a woman who really knows how to mourn," Tony said, looking at Richard again with his head tipped. "It can help the rest of the family if they see someone else doing it right." After a moment he added, "It can be hard for people to release their feelings, Mr. Cardinal. A loss like this," he said, "But it's a very important part of the goodbye process."

"Is she an actress or something?" Richard said.

"No. Well, not exactly," Tony said. "But trust me, she's done a lot of funerals. She's a real pro." He was quiet. "I'm not going to tell you that she's cheap, but it might be just what you're looking for," he said. "Even with a small showing, it would be a very memorable funeral."

Richard hesitated. "What are we talking here?" he said.

"Well, first, Mr. Cardinal, I want you to understand that Sorrentino and Williams doesn't get a cut of this. I'm only telling you about it, about her, because I know you loved your wife very much, and I think this might help." He looked away. A moment later he looked back and said, "Right now I think her fee is five hundred dollars for a half-hour visit," he said. "That includes a consultation beforehand."

"Gosh," Richard said. "I don't know."

"Eleanor's policy was very good, as you know, Mr. Cardinal," he said. "You'll be getting quite a bit back after all the funeral expenses. Think about it," he said. "Like I say, it might help things along," he said. "She's the best in Upstate New York. I know that."

"Okay," Richard said softly. "I'll think about it."

As Richard stood to leave, Tony wrote down a number on a piece of paper and handed it over to him. "Call her if you want to, Mr. Cardinal. It doesn't help with your numbers problem, but a good mourner can go a long way," he said.

Richard nodded.

When he got to the door, Tony added, "No one will ever have to know that she was hired."

Richard arranged to meet with her at Sammy's Café the next morning at ten o'clock, the day before the funeral. She was driving in from Syracuse. He thought there would be more to do after Eleanor died, but she'd made prearrangements and there wasn't much left to do at all. There was nothing. All morning, from five o'clock, he couldn't shake the terrible sensation that he was forgetting something. It came in panicky waves, like terror, like when he and Eleanor were young, and they'd had a small dog, and he'd see that someone had left the front door wide open.

She was exotic-looking, maybe forty, and he knew it was her from the moment she walked in. She had wavy black hair and soft curves. Her eyes were large and almost black. She was wearing red lipstick and a sparkly silver scarf that looked as if it had been knitted from tiny metal wires.

"You must be Richard," she said with a deep voice and an accent that he hadn't noticed on the phone. "I'm Dalia," she said, smiling and extending her hand.

He stood and shook her hand. Her perfume smelled spicy, like thyme and cloves.

As she sat down she said, "I'm sorry about your wife. It's very hard," she said. "I've lost people, and I know." She gestured for the waiter, then ordered a cup of coffee.

It bothered him to hear anyone say this. He'd lost people too—his mother, his father, his brother, many friends—but losing your wife of over forty years: she didn't know. Didn't know at all. "She wasn't in very much pain," he said, "and not for long."

"That's comforting," Dalia said.

"I guess," he said. "You take what you can get."

"I read the obituary," she said.

The waiter came over with her coffee, and a tiny silver pitcher of cream.

"It was a very nice obituary," she said, "very nice," pouring the cream into the coffee. It exploded into small clouds in the cup. "It seems like her happy something was being something," she said. "She didn't work," she said. "Is that right?"

"That's right," Richard said. "Well, not out of the house."

He told her all about Eleanor: how she'd married young, to a doctor, and how she found out she'd lost him the same day she found out she was pregnant with their son Bobby. He told her how they'd raised Bobby together, and had two children of their own, Annie and Jane, and how they lived on a quiet street in Whitesboro for all their life together. How Eleanor went to church every Sunday. How she had a sparkle in her eye, a keen wit that could make people laugh until they cried, and how she had a warmth in her like he'd never seen in any other person.

Dalia kept her eyes on him as he spoke, nodding gently. She was a striking woman, anyone would notice, and he could see people in the café sneaking glances at her. When she was out of questions, she smiled and said, "I can tell that you really loved her."

"I loved her," Richard said. "Yes."

She reached over and touched his hand for a moment. He had the feeling, then, like he might start to cry. He cleared his throat and gave her the check from his jacket pocket.

"I won't be seeing you after the funeral," she said. "But I want you to know that I'll do my best to honor your wife."

Richard looked down for a moment, then back to her dark eyes. He said, "If anyone asks—"

"Most people don't ask, Mr. Cardinal," she said. "But if they do— if anyone does ask—I could say that I knew her from church," she said. "Would that be okay?"

"Yes," Richard said. "That would work," he said.

He didn't know the exact moment he'd lost Eleanor. But it wasn't the moment she died. He knew that. The last few weeks in the hospital, most of the time she'd thought he was Albert Einstein. He felt vaguely flattered by this association, until Annie pointed out that it probably had something to do with his hair. The rest of the time she thought he was her first husband. They wouldn't let him go into the dialysis room with her, but from the hallway outside he heard the machine sputtering as it washed her blood. He heard her screaming, too; they had to sedate her. When the dialysis didn't work the second time, the doctors started to say that it was unlikely that her kidney function would return. More and more they were using the term *quality of life*. As in, "We can keep her alive—we're good at that—but you have to consider her quality of life, Mr. Cardinal." He hated the stupid phrase. Wasn't living, any living, always of a higher quality than the alternative? She'd been sick for a long time. He knew that she was going to die. None of it was a surprise. But what he hadn't considered, somehow—through her sickness, through their whole long life together—was that he would be the one who would have to say *when*.

Annie hadn't wanted to give up. She'd found case studies online about kidney function returning, liver cancer going into remission. She'd printed out the studies, highlighted sections. She begged him to let them keep trying the dialysis for another week. Maybe she would be one of those people who beat the odds? She could have more time. A week. A month. A few months, maybe. In the end it was a simple question from a nurse that helped him make the decision. "Is she still capable of experiencing joy?" the nurse had asked him. He looked at Eleanor in the bed, lost. Short beige hair. Rasps of breath. Thrashing. He signed the papers right then. Within an hour they'd moved her to a quiet room in a quiet wing of the hospital, where they set her up on a morphine drip. The doctor had told him that this was how most people die now. A far cry from the death he'd imagined in his youth, death like his father's, where you drop dead of a heart attack in your sleep. This now death was laborious, blown and terrifying to watch. The work it took to stop breathing. Nothing to do in that room. Everyone wanted to be the one to keep the wash-cloth on her forehead cold.

On the morning of the funeral Annie would not look him in the eye. He understood that she would be mad at him for a very long time, possibly forever. He felt ashamed and guilty the way he did when he'd been too harsh with her when she was a young child. Bobby and Jane seemed to be managing okay, but there was a blankness about Annie that was disconcerting. When she saw Eleanor in the casket for the first time she didn't even cry. "It doesn't look like her," she'd said.

"I don't know," Richard said. "I think they did a pretty good job," he said.

Annie stood there quietly. After a while, "I wonder if anyone will ever love me that much again," she said.

"I love you that much, Annie," he said.

"I know," she said. "I know you do."

People came in slowly at first, then in a big wave, all kneeling quickly at the casket, talking to Richard and the kids, then taking a seat in one of the pews to wait for the funeral service. Richard spoke to people he hadn't seen in years, Eleanor's body there in his peripheral vision all the while.

"Oh, Dick," her sister Gloria said. "She's in a better place now," she said. She was crying. "She's dancing in heaven now."

He held her in his arms, irritated that she'd say something like this. It occurred to him that he probably wouldn't see her as much anymore. He was surprised to find himself hoping that he still would.

Things were slowing down, it must have been a couple hours into the wake, when Tony passed through, caught Richard's eye, and nodded his head. Richard looked around. A minute later, Annie was focused on something, and when he turned and looked, he saw that Dalia had arrived, and she was walking to the casket. His face burned with heat and he felt a rush of adrenaline.

Annie kept staring at Dalia as though she were trying to place her.

Dalia kneeled quietly at the casket. Richard kept his eyes on her. She was wearing a tasteful black dress, a long gauzy sweater, and the same sparkly scarf she'd had on the day before. After a few minutes kneeling, she began to rock softly. She started to weep. Richard felt himself begin to sweat. Some moments passed like this, then she made a show of taking a handkerchief from her purse. Her hands were trembling as she held it to her face.

Annie kept glancing at her as she spoke to Gloria. Finally, she gestured toward the casket, then Gloria was looking too. They both took a seat in the first pew. Richard stood there dumbly, unsure of what to do, then he sat down next to them.

Dalia was still kneeling, but the pitch of her crying had started to rise. Then she started to moan. A few people had come in, Richard's cousin and his wife from Buffalo, and they were standing, waiting to pay their respects. When Dalia rested her head on the casket, Richard saw them exchange a glance.

People behind him were whispering. He heard Gloria say, "Who is that woman?" to Annie. Annie shrugged but didn't break her glance.

Now Dalia started sobbing, her rib cage shaking as she leaned over the casket. After a few moments, she straightened a bit, and then took both of her hands and silently grabbed at the hair on the top of her head. A hush came over the room when she did this. Everyone was watching. He'd made a mistake. Oh, he'd made a terrible, terrible mistake. Everyone would know that he did this. He'd made his wife's funeral a circus, a joke.

She unwound the silver scarf from her neck and let it fall to the ground. It pooled around her, twinkled like liquid in the light. A moment later she crawled from the kneeling bench onto the floor beside it. There, she lowered her head to the ground and stretched her arms out in front of her. She continued sobbing, her forehead to the ground. After a while, "Come back," she cried out softy. Then, "Please come back," she cried out again.

Hearing this, Annie started to weep uncontrollably. She buried her head in Richard's chest. "Mom," she cried. "Mom."

Richard put his arms around her and held her tightly. "I know," he said. "I know." It was the first time he'd held her this way in years. Her hair smelled clean, like honey, just the way it did when she was a girl. He closed his eyes and shifted his weight so that he could steady her.

Over by the casket, Dalia's hair was disheveled. She was still on the floor, wailing as he'd never heard someone do before. Her sounds were deep and inhuman. The room was silent, and he understood that everyone was staring, watching her. He turned to see that behind him, the funeral parlor was completely full. The pews were full, and people were standing all along the wall in the back too.

Several of their friends had made the trip from Florida. The kids' old friends had come too. Joni and Steve, who'd lived next door many years ago. All of their nieces and nephews had come: Lisa and Frank and Olivia. Josephine, Elena, Heather, and even Victor. They'd all flown in with their spouses. They had all gotten so big. Not big—old. Some of them were starting to go gray, even. Their niece Isabella came in all the way from California with her young daughter. The child had been doing fine, running about oblivious to where she was, but now she was crying too. So many people were crying, sobbing. Richard stood and went near the coffin. Eleanor was there in the pale blue dress that she'd picked to wear. Her best color. Richard's heart was doing unusual things in his chest. "Come on, now," he started to say, lifting Dalia to her knees. He bent down, tried to speak quietly in her ear. "That's enough now," he said. "You can stop now," he said. "Please," he said. "Please just stop."

But Annie was there beside him. "Dad," she said, looking in his eyes. "Leave her alone." She was not talking quietly, and he knew that everyone could hear her. Aside from some crying sounds, and the sounds of people shifting to see, the funeral parlor was nearly silent. Dalia looked up at him. He expected to see a different expression in her face, one of trickery or deceit, but her eyes were dim and blurry and had in them only a vague sparkle of recognition. Her face was red and covered with tears. He wondered then, who she'd lost, and when, and why it was still so potent. Could grief remain so raw as this forever, and were we all professional mourners clawing our way from one loss to the next?

"She loved Mom," Annie said. She was pulling him back to his seat.

He looked out at all the people filling the funeral parlor. So many of them were wiping their eyes. Others were holding each other. They'd all loved her. Still loved her. They came all this way because they really loved her.

"It's okay, Dad," Annie whispered.

And he realized, then, that he was crying too. He felt himself letting go, and he allowed himself to sink deeper into this feeling. His eyes went to Dalia's scarf, which was there on the floor next to where he was standing. He watched it sparkle in the light for a moment, then his mind went past the scarf, and past everyone's faces, and out into the night, to the sparkling city, and to the whole world that was beyond the city. He thought of how somewhere, right now, there were other people standing where he was standing, doing exactly what he was doing—saying goodbye to the very thing that they loved the most. He thought of how he was with them all in a way, and how, in a way, they were all here with him, too.

ACKNOWLEDGMENTS

My gratitude goes to all the people who have supported and encouraged my writing in their own various ways through the years.

Thank you to all the editors who accepted my work for publication, including: Greg Browderville, Vanessa Cuti, Scott Garson, Roxane Gay, S. Afzal Haider, Odette Heideman, Brandon Hodson, John T. Irwin, Lee Johnson, Terry L. Kennedy, Michael Koch, David Leavitt, Matthew Limpede, Dinty W. Moore, Anna Schachner, Ronald Spatz, Brandon Taylor, and Andrew Tonkovich. Special thanks also to the late C. Michael Curtis for his feedback and encouragement over the years.

Thank you to Elizabeth Evans, and the University of Arizona Poetry Center for its support.

Many thanks to my mentors: Arthur Flowers, Sheila Kohler, Doug Baur, Jim Krusoe, and especially to Amy Hempel, whose work changed my life. Special thanks to Aimee Bender for her guidance, generosity, and genuine kindness.

Thank you to Zibby Owens for believing in my work and for bringing this book into the world, and to Jordan Blumetti for his smart and thoughtful editing. Additional thanks to Anne Messitte, Kathleen Harris, Sherri Puzey, Diana Tramontano, Katie Teas, and everyone on the Zibby Books team. And to Anna Morrison for the beautiful cover design.

Thank you to Leigh Newman for the wise edits, enthusiasm, and encouragement.

Thank you to the Zibby Books authors, everyone from the Bennington Writing Seminars, and to the wonderful writing group from 30B.

Special thanks also to Mary Otis, Jill McCorkle, and Taylor Koekkoek.

Thank you to my agent, Julia Kenny, for believing in me, advocating for me, and for all the many things she did to help make this happen.

Sincere thanks to Marilyn Jacobs for her insight and wisdom.

Heartfelt thanks to my friends and family, especially my sister, Vicki, for being there for me every step of the way.

Very special thanks to my husband, Steve, for always believing in me, and keeping me going; and to my beautiful daughter, Sophie, for inspiring me every day, and for being my brightest light.

And for my mother, Dolores Jones, who gave me everything—you are never not with me.

About the Author

Mary Jones's stories and essays have appeared in many journals, including *Electric Literature's Recommended Reading*, *Subtropics*, *EPOCH*, *Alaska Quarterly Review*, *Columbia Journal*, *The Hopkins Review*, *Gay Mag*, *The Normal School*, *Epiphany*, *Santa Monica Review*, *Brevity*, and elsewhere. The recipient of a summer prose fellowship from the University of Arizona Poetry Center, her work has been cited as notable in *The Best American Essays* and appeared in *The Best Microfiction 2022*. She holds an MFA from Bennington College and teaches fiction writing at UCLA Extension. Originally from Upstate New York, she lives in Los Angeles.